SPLENDID ANATOMIES

SPLENDID ANATOMIES

stories

Allison Wyss

velizbooks.com

Splendid Anatomies

copyright © 2022 by Allison Wyss

All rights reserved. No part of this book may be used or reproduced in any manner whatsoever without written consent from the publisher, except for brief quotations for reviews.

Veliz Books' titles are available through our website and our primary distributor, Small Press Distribution, 800.869.7533.
For personal orders, catalogs, or other information, write to info@velizbooks.com.

For further information, write

    Veliz Books
    P.O. Box 961273
    El Paso TX 79996
    velizbooks.com

ISBN: 978-1-949776-11-9

Cover photo by Korey Rowswell of his work "High Lonesome," a mixed textile sculpture. All rights reserved.

Cover design by Veliz Books

For Paul and Averil

SPLENDID ANATOMIES

You're Perfect As You Are	3
The Seamstress and the Spider	23
Only Real Art Lasts Forever	29
The Vortex	50
Dr. Francis Longfellow Hendrix	56
Garden	69
Sleep Birds	71
Fishing	74
Roar	77
Nutsacks in Space	108
From the Multiverse Chronicles	111
FastDog Security	116
The Mole	152
Curse the Toad	155
Boobman	162
Snow White Alive	185
Acknowledgements	193
About the Author	195

You're Perfect As You Are

This is my natural nose. You can look through all my old baby pictures to satisfy yourself that it is. The same nose that won Miss Cutesy-Pie of the Week on Channel 17 News at Five. The same nose that got skinned, but did not scar, when Jared Castlemann pushed me into the wall on Field Day in eighth grade. It's the same nose that Danny Pinkerton kissed by mistake, with his eyes closed and the canoe wobbling, on Crooked Lake. (Pretty soon after that, he found my mouth.)

My mouth is not natural, or the skin around my eyes. My figure is not at all like nature meant for it to be by now. Thanks to Dr. L.

But my nose is my own and the same and all me. It's all me!

...9:00-9:15: Arrive at the office. (But not today!)

I'm not at work today but home, in my new home. I just bought a condo. A two-bedroom unit, 825 square feet. Dr. L. gave me a couple days off to move in and get settled.

It's boob season anyway, so I'm less important at the office. Not that I can't sell boobs. Dr. L. gave me some nice round C cups. On the big side of a C. More would be too much for my frame. But who knows? If styles change, we'll change them too.

Boobs were big for a while. I mean big boobs were big. But Dr. L. correctly assessed it was a short-lived fad, that time. So I didn't go under again, just wore some fakes. I don't show cleavage at work. I'm a professional, after all.

...9:15-10:00: Make coffee, go over the day's agenda. (Hmm. Same, I think.)

I'm pretty much settled into the condo. At least physically. Furniture-wise and regarding unpacking. The couch, the chairs, the coffee table—all placed just so. Dishes are stacked in the cupboards, though I might change that, might put the glasses over the sink and keep the plates directly above the dishwasher, instead. Canned food is in the corner cabinet—harder to reach but I don't get at it much anyway. A bright bowl of dimpled oranges rests on the counter.

Dr. L.'s nose is straight, with a graceful, swooping mustache that runs like a stream of water from each nostril. I blow the white from it after lunch each day and after his afternoon break, but I don't mark *that* on my day planner.

Only my Roomba is still packed up, in its original box on my living room floor. My condo has an open floor plan, kitchen unfolding to breakfast nook, to dining area, to living space—perfect for the Roomba.

I slide my fingernails through the tape on the box, pull out a cube of Styrofoam and crack it open like an egg.

The thing is kind of creepy. Like a giant beetle stuck on its back with its legs all wiggly. It's kind of grotesque.

Ah, no, it's not. Not when I flip it. It's cute. He's a cute little fella!

...10:00-11:30: Sell the nose! (Check for breakage—those movers... Monitor the Roomba, organize the kitchen.)

I don't do anything special to sell the nose. I just sit at my desk. I have a bowl of hard candies that I offer to potential clients. I suck these discreetly, quiet on my tongue when the moment calls for it. Or a gentle suck to push my lips and highlight my cheekbones. I answer the phone if it rings, pretend to call local celebrities—just minor ones. I make small talk. Depending on which seat the client chooses, I angle my chair and then my face, just so. I draw their eyes to my perfect nose.

My job includes a bit of light accounting, as well, but not in front of clients, because apparently my nose crinkles when I crunch numbers. Dr. L. pointed it out and offered to relieve me of the duty, but I said I'd keep it. And sometimes I work crossword puzzles, careful not to let my brow wrinkle or my nose squish over the difficult ones.

The Roomba is all face but no features, just a flat disc, and I don't know how to point it. I put it to the middle of the floor, press the start button, and hop out of its way.

Zoom-zoom, let's go little fella!

And it's the most popular nose in all of Indianapolis, Dr. L. says. He says it's made him a million bucks, and so easy, so easy. He says this as he swipes his thumb across it, oh-so-gently. He stands above my desk, and I prop my elbows on the appointment book.

Or sometimes he says it as he presses my head down into his lap, oh-so-gently. When he runs my nose along the underside of his penis. "My million dollar nose," he says then. Moans it, really. And I'll joke about the value of his dick and how it belongs to me. But really the nose is mine and the penis is his. It's just a game we play.

I used to always watch TV while I vacuumed, with the volume way up, so I flip it on now, even though it's just game shows and soap operas this time of day. It's good to have background noise as I sort and re-position dishes. Otherwise it's just the whoosh-whoosh and hum of my little buddy on the floor.

There, the plates are better in the cabinet above the dishwasher. But the movers just threw together all the canned foods. Soups in with beans in with vegetables. Can't let that stand, so I sort the cans into food groups first, then step back to see my work. Then I sort them further into types of meals—for when I'm in a hurry, for when I'm in recovery, for when I'm sad. Or the biggest set, I hope, for when I'm feeling most myself.

When I first walked through the door to Dr. L.'s office, leading with the nose, as always, Dr. L. was sitting on top of the receptionist desk which was covered in crinkled papers and pen caps, even cracker crumbs and dust bunnies.

He scooted forward off the desk, pulling down a sprinkle of debris that fell at his ankles.

"I'm looking for Dr.—"

"—No! No, I couldn't possibly help you."

"You don't know the doctor?"

"I am him." He was staring at me, at my nose, with this charged intensity that, frankly, I get all the time.

"Then you can help me," I said.

"No. No, I couldn't possibly. You're perfect as you are."

My eyes started upward, but I stopped them from rolling, with effort. I said, "I believe you're looking for a receptionist."

"Oh, yes, of course."

He led me into his office and asked the usual questions about experience, of which I had plenty, and also about goals and professionalism and how I'd found him.

It was before he offered the job, but after I became sure that he would offer it, that he leaned forward and lowered his voice. "Would it be all right if I touched your nose?"

"Excuse me?"

"It's real, right?" He put his hand in front of my face, but not too close.

I was rather desperate for the job, I can admit that. This was eight years ago. I'd been divorced for two and working at the bleak old chiropractor's office across town.

But that's not why I consented. I knew I would value his expert opinion on a pretty nice asset of mine. Also, Dr. L. is quite alluring.

He held his thumb and forefinger out, pinched the very top, and then ran his fingers, slowly, to the tip. He prodded around that, worked his way back up. Stroked the bridge with each finger. One, by one, by one, of both hands. Sighed.

Then he pulled pincers from his desk drawer and said, "May I? It won't hurt." I nodded. He held them, cold and surgical, to each nostril, turned a dial, then studied the metal, wrote something down. "I can do that," I think he mumbled. Then he glanced up. "Can you start Monday?"

...11:30-12:30: Early lunch. (As if I'm even hungry yet....)

Ooh! The Roomba nips at my ankle! A light tap sends him back into the open space.

Dr. L.'s wife wouldn't play a game like ours because she is stern about her property and her body and what's hers and what isn't. I don't know this for sure but extrapolate it from the stories Dr. L. tells of her. She's a software engineer but still dresses well. Also she won't let Dr. L. change her appearance, but only uses him to stay exactly the same age—pulling up the skin of her face, tucking in pouches of her abdomen. I hear this in her voice on the phone when she calls the office to check up on him.

The Roomba has stopped, stalled. The instructions don't tell me much except to put him down and let him go. Except, well, it's hard to know which way to face it. I mean, it doesn't have a face—or just a blank one. No nose to point in a direction. Maybe he just needs some attention. When I put him back down, he scoots away.

Several times a day, Dr. L. will call me into his patient consultations. I walk to my mark on the carpet and point my nose at a predetermined spot on the wall behind him so I can answer some silly question he invents.

The client sits politely while I answer but will often speak before the door has closed behind me. "Can you do that nose? Her nose? Can you do that one on me?"

Then he leans forward, I imagine, touches the tissue of it, prods at the bone, as he did to me that first day. It's an act for them. For me it was real.

My nose gets stuffy or runny sometimes, and then Dr. L. says to go home and get better. So I do, and he still pay me for the days I spend in bed or on the couch dozing through soap operas, *Animal Planet*, and *The Price Is Right*. He sends the temp agency receptionist to my apartment with scheduling questions and hot soup and bright orange specialty Robitusson. He sends her with ribbon-wrapped slippers and fuzzy robes and silly romance novels. He tells me on the phone he's sending kisses with her. But she's always too prim to deliver.

And the few days the temp agency has sent men to Dr. L.'s office, he's sent nothing to me. No kisses or soup or flowers or scheduling questions.

...12:30-1:00: Back at it. See to clients. (Not much left to organize.)

Today, I'm not sick. Just home to finish up my unpacking and settling, though there's not much to do.

My condo is 825 square feet. I own the inside surfaces of the outer walls but not what's behind them. Any spot the Roomba reaches, I own it. And when he bumps a wall and spins out another way, that means I don't own that part that he can't get to.

At least I think so. I should ask Denny. He's my realtor.

...1:00-1:15: Administrative. (Let's see what Denny has to say!)

Hi Denny,

Just a quick question. If I paint my walls, do I still own the original color, or do I forfeit that in creating a new inside surface?

Please advise,

Ursula

Hi Denny,

Hoping you can help me out with something. Which slice of the hallway is mine? Do I own the space in front of my door or a long stripe down the center?

Thanks for your help!

Ursula

Hi Denny,

Ha ha! I'm wondering about the carpet too! When I

clean it, do I increase or decrease the property value? After all, the dirt I pull will go in the trash and leave my possession and ownership. Or does it?

Any help appreciated!

Ursula

...1:15-1:45: Administrative. (Reconsider decor.)

The movers put my green vase in the kitchen, but it doesn't go there. It's pretty enough to sit on the end table, to sparkle in the sunshine from the window.

It was only a week or so in that Dr. L. brought me some powder for my nose. Blow, you know. Cocaine. He was so excited by it. Turned on. I played dumb like I didn't know what to do, like I was scared, but like I trusted him.

I don't know why that old instinct kicked in. It's a survival thing, I think.

So I let him seduce me, like I didn't know it was coming. Like I didn't start it, didn't lay down a scent for him to sniff up. Just for fun, you know.

The thing that interests me about Dr. L. is his power and the way he's manipulated by it. He thinks he controls more than he does, and it's adorable. And so for me, there's a thrill in pretending.

The Price Is Right is droning on. But look at the model! She's caressing a box of soap, and if the contestant knows the price, they can putt from a closer line. The model's hand is open like a flower petal, curling the air around each product. She's young and she's gorgeous with a smile like sunshine. Except look at the nose on her! So wide!

Poor girl. But look how well she's done and good for her.

Some women would hate the cliché of sleeping with their married boss. But I kind of like that aspect—it takes the pressure off.

Anyway, I'm not a total coke-head or something. Just, if it's at a party. It used to be always at a party, and I used to go to a lot of parties. And if I don't have to buy my own or make any promises and if I trust the fellow who offers me some. Then. Well, what's the harm in just a little?

There's this thing about pretending. It used to be I couldn't pretend, and I couldn't because what I pretend now was real. I was just a doll, and I belonged to someone as a doll, they thought. It wasn't pretend, and if anyone could turn that off, it wasn't me.

Dear Ursula,

Actually, since there are 326 identical condominiums in your building, you own 1/326th of every single atom in the hallway. You also own 1/326th of every atom in the studs of the outside walls of your unit.

Painting your walls will not affect the amount of space that you own. It may however affect the value of your home.

Vacuuming is a good practice but it will not change the property value.

Hope this helps!

Dennis

...1:45–2:00: *Administrative, clients, etc. (Respond!)*

> Hello Dennis,
> I don't understand at all about the painting. You said the surface is mine—doesn't the surface change as I paint it?
> Thanks in advance for your help.
> Ursula

...*2:00-2:15: Fun time with Dr. L. (Or take stock of life, yet again.)*

My condo is 825 square feet and all carpet but the bathroom, all at the mercy of the Roomba. The faceless robot bustles from one wall to another, a swath of fresh cleanness opening behind him, brushing the carpet fibers into smooth ribbons running one way and then another.

What parts of anybody's body are real anyway? Nothing is original. All cells replaced, year after year after year. Wax off eyebrows, pencil in new ones. Yank the hair out by its soft and wiggly roots.

Those peaked-at-prom stereotypes of pretty girls are just plain wrong. Maybe my life is not so exciting as those nerdy girls who fly off around the country or the corporate broads making ba-jillions of dollars.

But my life is sure better now than it was in high school. I did not peak then. I can handle sex better (and enjoy it!) for one thing. Also, I do what I want now. I'm very independent.

Those power suit execs—the ones who used to be nerds. I met loads of them at my 20-year reunion last fall.

They don't have the freedom I have. They're *still* trying to impress someone.

Swept up in your job or what people think or whatever. It's like a bad marriage, when you lose even yourself, and *there* is real loneliness. Let me tell you about loneliness then, with even yourself gone and your freedom and no one to love you anyway.

Thank god I'm through with that. Poor dears.

Once I faked a pimple to get the day off from Dr. L. It worked, and I went ice-skating. What a day!

Dr. L. is better than a husband. I get this whole space to myself and my nose and myself to myself, and still he loves me.

The Ursula-500. That's what we named it. My nose.

But then, mid-sniff, mid-rail, on that very first time Dr. L. gave me blow, I wondered if I could trust this guy. I mean, *really*. Of course, I couldn't. And I was glad to realize it, even so late in the game, and that made me trust myself more.

I'm the one I should trust, really. Me and this natural-born nose. Plain as it is on my face. And not plain at all, not really.

Oh! The Roomba has found me again! It bumps the couch beneath my knees, then sweeps toward the opposite wall.

Now it's some soap opera on TV. A woman dressed to kill, in someone's elegant living room. The emotion on her face, long pauses, intense stares. And graceful tears sliding away from that nose again. The wide one.

The trend is alarming.

I don't have illusions about Dr. L. and me. I still date, after all.

Like that Denny fellow. Maybe him. He's a cutie.

Mrs. L. calls me twice a week to check on the doctor's habit. I don't answer her except in a code devised by me which I've never explained to her. Still, I know that she gets it.

Yes, yes. My nose is real and it always will be. He can't touch it. Won't touch it. That same nose that brings me breath after breath. Filters it. Warms it. Connects me to life.

Some other bits. Well, what the heck is this piece of skin right here? It's still me, I suppose, but the smoothness of it? The flat run? Well, it wasn't always like that. It was smooth when I was young. And then time crinkled it. Dr. L. drew it smooth again.

But that makes it sound too easy. Like he just pulled out a tiny iron and board and with a hiss of steam and a little steady pressure....

Really, it hurt. And between crinkled and smooth, there's a lot of ugly. Other kinds of black and blue and torn-up ugly.

Also lots of staying home from work, but still getting paid. And watching *The Price Is Right* in the silk bathrobe some days, some days in the fuzzy one. And the down slippers that a temporary receptionist with a totally ordinary nose and no punch to her kissless lips delivered to me in my old, rented apartment.

Silly little Roomba. All face, all surface, but without any eyes or ears or mouth. How do you point it if there is no nose?

> Ursula,
> You will still own the underlying surface, even if you paint over it. However, accessing that surface, once covered, may prove difficult.
> Dennis

Ugh. That makes no sense!

...2:15-2:30: Confirm appointments. (Shower and think about that weird email.)

I step into the steam of a shower, my first shower in this space that I own. It's too hot, because I don't know the knobs yet, but then I get it right.

"No, you're perfect as you are," is the first line of Dr. L.'s favorite sales pitch.

He then lets the woman slowly convince him that he has no idea—that it's not his opinion that matters, but her own.

On slow afternoons, he practices the ploy on me. I play all the roles: aging starlet, haggard housewife, chubby 23-year-old. "Oh, I couldn't possibly," he always starts.

The game ends with a tap on the nose and a pinch on the ass. I shriek, in character, before falling into his arms.

Then he locks the door, while I clear a spot for us—on my desk, usually.

Why do I listen to Dr. L.? Because he is a part of me. If this nose is me, this one I've never touched, then he is too. Him telling me to go home, to lose weight, to tighten—just barely—my grip on his penis, it's the same as me deciding for myself.

Or is it? I'll have to think more on that one. It seems so obvious, yet there must be more to it.

Dr. L.'s face is like sunshine—except there is no sunshine. It's just sparkles and reflections.

...2:30-2:45: See to clients, make fresh coffee. (Respond!)

> Dennis,
> So if I pull down the wallpaper in the bathroom, do I gain property or lose it?
> Ursula

...2:45-3:00: Client bullshit. (And yet again.)

> Dear Dennis,
> How precisely does the atom split? Do I get electrons or protons or neutrons? Also, wouldn't this process be categorized as nuclear fission?
> Please advise,
> Ursula

...3:00-3:15: Maybe a snack? (And where is the messenger from Dr. L.?)

I deserve a treat. So I eat an orange, but slowly, to make it last. I press a spoon concave against the peel. Juice spurts. Then the peel works off in small leathery patches. I break open each segment to see the tiny tentacles before popping it into my mouth and juicing it with my tongue.

Dr. L. hired movers for me. By proxy, he's the perfect husband.

Zip zip, it's my little pal crossing in front of my feet. The drops of water on the floor from my shower don't pick up like the bits of cardboard dust from all the boxes.

I suppose, it's not bad logic, the Roomba. Go until you hit something, until your nose is pressed flat to a wall or a window or the flat palm of your lover's hand. Then bounce back, adjust directions, and try again.

> Dear Ursula,
> Perhaps I didn't use the best metaphor. Instead of atoms, you should think of your ownership in terms of shares. It's as though each owner in your building owns one share of the common area. You don't own a particular piece. Instead you share each piece.
> I've attached a document that explains this concept in more detail.
> Dennis

...*3:15–3:45: Correspondence. (One more.)*

> Dear Dennis,
> Thank you for your patient explanations. I understand now. However, I am still unsure if it would be okay for

me to place a welcome mat outside of my front door, in the hallway. If I don't own that space, I don't think I should. And yet my neighbor has done it.
Your prompt reply is much appreciated.
Ursula

Probably I should stop bothering him.

After the orange, I grab a cookie. I follow the Roomba into my bedroom and crumble the cookie directly in front of him. He deserves a snack, too.

My phone buzzes, and it's Dr. L. "Just checking in," he says.

"Oh, well I'm fine. How's the temp working out? What's her name?"

"Who, Pauline? Great, actually. She's a pretty girl. Got a knack for it."

"Will you send her by?"

"Um."

"You don't have to."

"—No, it's fine."

"I mean, I shouldn't expect."

"Ursula, it's been a hectic day."

"I'm so sorry for mentioning it."

"What with you gone...."

"I shouldn't have assumed. I just wanted to make sure I wouldn't be in the shower or something. But if she's not coming, then I don't have to worry."

There's a long pause when he might be listening to something else. "Ursula, I should let you go."

The good thing about Dr. L. is he never pretended about why he hired me and what my job is. It's scheduling, too. But he never pretended it wasn't also to sell noses, as well as eye work, chin work, boob work—you name it. The playing house part, the sex, is not officially the job.

And on TV, another commercial. Another nose. They are getting wider. The nostrils. The bridge. Lips shrink and swell, I know this. As do boobs. Butts. I don't care.

But noses? Noses?

Noses.

The Roomba is still at it. He crosses his own path again, drawing over himself, erasing himself. He bumps one way. Bumps another. Searching searching searching for the last patch of cardboard dust. It's there, right in the middle, but he can't find it.

He'll never get anywhere. He's just buzzing around.

Which way is his nose?

...3:45-4:00   General   receptionist   duties,   crossword, administrative. (Dennis.)

> Dear Dennis,
> Because if I had a welcome mat.... Well, if you would stop by, Denny, you would know that you are welcome. Perhaps, Denny, you could stop by sometime? For some coffee or a glass of wine?
> Sincerely,
> Ursula

...4:00-4:30: Client appreciation. (Watch TV and pace the room. Will someone come?)
I never watch TV, so I don't even know the commercials. All new faces. But there's that nose again. I am not a shallow person, but Jesus Christ that nose is ugly!

...4:30-5:00: Can I call it a day?
There's someone at the door, and it must be Dr. L.'s messenger. After all, he has sent one! It must be Pauline.

Through the peephole, she's dressed like a temporary receptionist and holds the scheduling book in her hand along with a grip of roses. I catch her sniffing them. I swing the door open, and she pulls them down.

Wide nose pops out. I know it. I know it. From *The Price Is Right*, from *Days of Our Lives*, from the Noxzema commercial.

"Miss Carston?" she says.

"Call me Ursula." I turn away from the nose, lead her through my foyer into the freshly swept living room. Satin ribbons of carpet woven into crosshatches under our feet.

The flowers are fuzzy blobs of color beneath her face, which is clear, too clear. That nose and its sweep. The slope of the skin stretched across it.

Then the patch of red moves upward, and she's pushing the roses at me. They are still fuzzy. They are in my hands.

I fill the green vase with water. It sparkles. And that splaying handful of red roses.

Then we sit. We open the schedule on the coffee table and she is across from me on the couch. Her panty-hosed knees point politely to the side. The nose, in profile, is like mine. Head on, facing me, it spreads. It flows to her cheeks like water, like tears.

I pencil a few changes, jot down a list of clients to call back. I manage to do it. I manage to think about my job and remember a particular client and the way she might be tricky.

But the whole time, I can't stop looking at it. She talks, and I can't hear the words, just the bobbing of that nose over her lips, the slight nostril flare or crinkling that comes with certain words. I don't know what those words are. It's not only beautiful—After all, it *is* beautiful!—and just like *The Price Is Right*, *Days of Our Lives*, the Noxzema commercial—but it's animated. It must be a natural nose.

Staring straight at the fullness of that thing, it's like there's a twig stuck to my face, an empty, skinny bone. My hand floats up, hovers like a mask, but I pull it down because hiding only makes it worse.

When she leaves, finally, when the Roomba draws a shiny line over her footprints in the carpet, I put my fingers to my face, and I pull away my nose. I feel the nose separate from me. I am apart from this nose. My face is smooth, but my nose is held apart in my hand.

The Seamstress and the Spider

—Do you know what a seamstress is?
—Yes, it's a dressmaker.
—Right.
—And I think she's very beautiful.
—Well, some are, but maybe not this one. Maybe that doesn't matter so much.
—Can't I think so?
—OK. For now, you can.
—Tell me the story.
—Once there was a seamstress who lived alone deep in the woods. She was a pretty good seamstress, though not a great one. She was young and still had a lot to learn.

One day the seamstress didn't have any dresses to make—it was a slow time of year—and so she decided to dust. It was a very crooked cottage that she lived in, and it had lots of funny corners. The seamstress was not much of a housekeeper, and cobwebs would fill those corners, one atop the other, until the house's edges were soft and round like pillows.

On this day, the seamstress dusted high and low, above the cupboards and under the stove. She dusted corner after corner until she reached the final, acute angle at the far end of her bedroom. There she found a single, beautiful spider web that stretched from the bedpost to the small knob on the lowest drawer of her bureau. The web's pattern was as intricate as fine lace, and it glistened in the sunlight. In the center was a majestic spider, covered head to foot in thick, black fur.

"Hello," said the seamstress.

"Well, hello," said the spider.

The seamstress was surprised when the spider returned her greeting but tried not to appear so. "You have a very fine web," she said. "What is it made of?"

"See for yourself," said the spider.

The seamstress touched her finger to the web, and it did not break. When she took a corner of it into her mouth and bit it very gently, she knew it was pure gold. She said, "With thread like this, I could sew for a queen."

"Oh could you now?" The spider chuckled. For, of course, she herself was a queen.

"What could I trade you for it?"

"There's nothing you could trade me for a web I spun out of my own self, dear." The spider spoke with regal disdain and held her furry chin high. "However, if you would sew me a blouse, a beautiful and perfect blouse, I could teach you to spin your own golden thread."

The seamstress agreed.

"But you must take care," the spider warned. "For if the blouse is not a good fit, I could not answer for my anger."

The seamstress shuddered, then set to work right away. She measured the spider and allowed her to choose from several fabrics that she had on hand. She cut the pieces with sure strikes of her shears. Then she settled herself behind her needle. She stitched late into the night, for, as you may know, setting in sleeves can be difficult, and this blouse required more than the usual number. The full moon tossed a dusty glow through her window. After sewing for a very long time, she laid the shirt flat. Then she tore out a seam and realigned the pieces. As the sun emerged between the trees, she tore out the same seam again and again, attempting to rework the final sleeve. No matter how many times she pulled the stitches and started over, the sleeve simply would not sit.

When day had altogether broken, the seamstress was still reworking the sleeve. She heard the spider moving about in the bedroom, and her frustration gave way to panic. The finicky sleeve—belligerent, she thought—fell to the floor. The seamstress kicked it hastily beneath a rug. Then she hunched over the blouse and quickly stitched shut the space where it should have been attached.

"Is it finished?" called the spider.

"Come see for yourself."

The spider scuttled into the room and snatched up the garment. She draped the blouse over her back and burrowed her head through the neck opening. She squirmed until one long, skinny arm, then another, popped through sleeves of the blouse. The third arm slithered through its slippery tunnel, then the fourth, the fifth. A sixth appendage was momentarily stuck in the wrong place, then adjusted. Awkwardly, arm number seven jutted into the remaining sleeve. The spider turned in a circle as the final limb sought its sheath.

"Something is wrong," the spider said. "Perhaps it's a bit twisted?"

"Can't you even dress yourself?" The seamstress spoke without thinking and, upon realizing her words, she clapped her hand to her mouth. "I mean—"

The spider glared. With her head fixed on the girl, she rotated her torso until it seemed an arm—or maybe several—would pop from the socket. "Remember our bargain, child. It's only good if it fits."

"Of course it fits," said the seamstress. And without another thought, she pulled a pair of scissors from her pocket and snipped the final arm from the spider's body.

The arm flopped onto the floor and wriggled for a moment. It was a hairy thing, and the blood that seeped from it was dark and thick.

—Then what?

—Well, the seamstress was worried the spider would be angry, so she gobbled her right up.

—No, tell me the real ending.

—That should be the real ending. Spiders are very nutritious. You should make sure to eat at least twelve spiders every year. I like them toasted and sprinkled with cinnamon.

—Gross.

—If you think so. You can let yours crawl in your mouth as you sleep.

—Grandma, tell me the real ending.

—The real one, Velma?

—Yes.

—It's very awful.

—I know it is.

—The seamstress didn't eat the spider, Velma. The spider ate the seamstress.

—How did she eat her?

—The spider bit off this finger. Then this one. Then, with her razor sharp teeth, the spider crunched through her elbow.

—Did the seamstress get away?

—Maybe she did. Maybe she lived the rest of her life with one arm, always sewing in circles.

—Maybe?

—Or maybe the spider spooned her eyes out of their sockets and munched them like meatballs. The seamstress wouldn't stop screaming, so the spider paused to devour her tongue. When her face was nothing but shreds, the spider ate her other arm and then her legs. The seamstress didn't die right away but was still thinking and screaming inside her head until the spider slurped her brain like noodle soup.

—Which ending is it, Grandma? I mean really.

—Or maybe she didn't get eaten at all. Maybe, instead, the spider scurried away and left the seamstress holding the extra leg, still wriggling.

—What did she do with it?

—She put it in her pocket.

—Maybe she got it to help with her sewing.

—Maybe she did.

Velma turned over in her bed and snuggled into her pillow. She closed her eyes but was still thinking about the seamstress and the spider.

—Grandma, did the seamstress have a name?

—Oh, she had one, all right, but it's been lost.

—How do you lose your name?

—She didn't lose it. The storytellers did.

—You lost it?

—Me? No. It was lost before I knew it. But that doesn't mean she didn't have one. Now go to sleep.

ONLY REAL ART LASTS FOREVER

FALL[1]

I walk in, and it's just body parts, full female ones, disassembled by lines drawn, pictures swirling, sliding, shimmering across white skin. A flickering snake tattoo with blue and teal scales slithers up from an ankle, coils between loose legs, drops into a pile at one breast. Then it stretches, yellow eyes gleam, and a cranberry tongue licks up her neck to tickle her ear. Live fingers twist and rub thighs covered in sunset. Those fingers are sprinkled with inky flowers, and vines climb around delicate arms. A bright nipple pops. Faeries dance around it.

Then I find a face in the patterns. It's Dolores, our old friend, eyes closed and barely breathing—I hold my breath to hear her quiet ones. She's smiling softly, calm under Poncho's humming needle.

---

1 But late. The trees are nearly bare.

"Oh shit, sorry." But I've already stood there too long. I didn't expect her to be naked. I pull my hands together, peel a bright petal of polish off one fingernail, and watch it waft to the floor. "I was just looking for—" Poncho keeps tattooing. Dolores never looks at me. I back out of Poncho's studio and into the main room of our tattoo shop for the rest of the day.

Later, I'm in the pool, flinging myself through the water. I count the strokes between breaths. 1-2-3-4-5. It's five years since Amy left, since I stayed here, with Poncho, to open the tattoo shop. The thoughts that float over my counting, behind the waterline—they aren't like other thoughts.

Usually it's Amy that floats in front of me when I swim. I see her hair like a river, rippling in a smooth ponytail down her back. Or I think about a design that I'm working on. Words and pictures, right at the waterline. I think of Poncho's paintings, too.

I didn't go with Amy because:

~~Love is not eternal.~~

WINTER[2]

I swim every day at the Y, except if I've got fresh punchings, and even then I only let a day or two pass. It's the best I ever feel. The ache in my arms and the tightness

---

[2] It's deep winter and snow is piled against the windows, but the pool is warm and steamy. The season doesn't matter at the natatorium because it only ever smells of chlorine. But Dubby likes the winter best, the constant warmth as she swims, the strong glass windows that hold out against the weather.

in my lungs. The way my thoughts hover at the waterline, safely away, just beyond my reach.

Poncho is my business partner, and he's the real thing, an artist. He closes his eyes when clients talk to him. Then, when they finish, he gets out his sketchbook and shows them what it is they want. Mostly I have clients flip through the book, and those are the clients that come to me, the kind who want to flip through the book.

But I'm good at some things, like predicting weight change and aging. All tattoos are affected by time, you can't help that, but you can make your drawings so they grow with the skin. So they don't look the same ten years later, or twenty, but they still make sense. Poncho doesn't see it that way. He makes something lasting every time.

Poncho does the people who are looking for real art, like Dolores. She doesn't come often, but when she appears, she and Poncho lock themselves in his tattoo room for days. Then she emerges more glorious than the last time. And Poncho is exhausted and relaxed, talkative and happy. She lets him draw whatever he wants on her. He just freestyles, and she never regrets letting him do it, I don't think.

I remember when Poncho was just Nick, before we all started calling him Poncho. My real name is Sara, but people mostly call me Dubby. It was my brother's nickname in high school, but then it got stuck to me, and I can't seem to shake it.

In the pool, I don't even count laps anymore, just strokes. I swim until I'm too tired to go further. And in my mind, I hold one of Poncho's paintings, or else one of his tattoos.

I didn't go with Amy because:

~~Only real things last forever.~~

I'm in the tattoo parlor on a slow afternoon. I'm sorting through our design books, pulling out pages that are ragged so I can redraw the pictures on fresh paper. The drawings are arranged by category except for a few of mine that Poncho has moved to the back. I can take a hint. I rip these out and don't redraw them.

Then suddenly it's Dolores at the door. She swings the top part of her body through the front entrance, her face bright, her fingers hooked on the door frame. I haven't seen her in months, not since I walked in on her, naked, in Poncho's studio.

"Poncho isn't here." Can't she read the wall? Five years ago, Poncho wrote our schedule there, and we still haven't changed it because the days and times won't wash off. He writes notes there, too, between the polaroids of his best work, always with a permanent marker. "He doesn't come in until three on Tuesdays."

"I know. I came to talk to you, Dubby." It's snowing outside, and Dolores wriggles out of a heavy coat. She looks unusually modest in flannel and long sleeves, but the top buttons are open and the skin between tattoos is pink and glowing.

"Don't tell Poncho, okay?" Dolores says. "I haven't been around because I've been seeing someone else. I want to come back to Poncho, only I just can't let him see the work I had done." This comes out in a rush before I have time to make any excuses or stop from hearing it.

I can't think how to make my face look or how I could possibly help Dolores. I'm good at keeping secrets, but sometimes knowing them is hard.

"It's just small, see?" Dolores lifts her shirt to her chin and points to a bird, low on her chest. It's only an inch long, but it's obviously not Poncho's work. "Do you think you could cover it? Or make it look like Poncho's?"

"Uh." It's what I do every day, draw Poncho's designs on skin. I fool most people, but I couldn't get anything past Poncho.

"Dubby, you have to." Dolores pushes her mouth into a pout that surprises me. Is she flirting? "I know you can do it."

"He's gonna know he never drew anything there." I put my finger on the bird, and her skin is hot beneath it. I jump back, tingling. I didn't mean to touch her.

Dolores doesn't flinch. She takes off her shirt, and I make a tracing of the bird—carefully—professionally. It's a red finch, quiet, nestled between two trolls on the inside of her breast.

Dolores is pretty, and she's nice to me—that's why I agree. Also, I must like a lost cause. Because there's no chance of this working, no chance of fooling Poncho. You can't make real art and then forget it.

Afterward, I catch a glimpse of Dolores's back as she dresses. "FOREVER." Five-inch black gothic, with green ocean waves swirling in front, obscuring and eroding the bottom from the F, the V, curling into both R's. It's beautiful. Then it vanishes as she pulls the shirt over her shoulders and tugs it down past her waist where it clings to her hips. Only that snake's tongue and a spray of violets peep over her collar. I don't know if it's her body or if it's Poncho's art that holds me.

But she's moving too slowly. I shake myself from the trance. "It's quarter to three," I say.

"Oh, better go! Thank you!"

"Come back next week, but *early*," I say as she scoots out the front door.

This is going to be hard.

Growing up, everybody wanted to be Poncho's friend, but I was the one who lived on his block and walked to school with him. In high school, when a dozen girls lined up to drive Poncho home every day, he'd still ride with me in my hundred-dollar Honda. He had a knack for tying the door closed with the seatbelt and guiding the windows up and down with both hands. He liked to talk to me about painting and getting out of Indiana, making some mark on the world. I never said much but always wanted the same things, something bigger than here, that would last.

Poncho went to art school in Chicago, a few hours away, and then pretty much starved for a year in New York. I was working in a comic book store mostly, drawing a lot and also getting heavy into tattoos. I got licensed, got pretty good at the tattoos, actually.

I was dreaming with Amy then, wrapped in her hair, tying her to me. We were saving for California. We would live in the sunshine, by the beach. Amy would teach first grade, and I would find some job or other. Love felt bigger than art, like it could outlive us both.

Then Poncho came home, looking beat-up and skinny. He was the real thing now, an artist, and he needed me. He and I opened Body of Art, and Amy went to California without me.

Dolores's tattoo. Poncho's going to know right away. If I can somehow manage to cover this bird for Dolores, what does it mean about Poncho? What does it mean about his art?

I leave the shop early, waiting just long enough for Poncho's glasses to unfog after he sweeps himself in the front door. I drive straight to the Y.

It's better in the pool. My armstrokes. Poncho's brushstrokes. 1-2-3-4-5. Except, today, instead of Amy, instead of Poncho's paintings, it's that piece of Dolores, that snake tongue uncoiling. It skims the water line in front of my fingers, twists half above and half below. It's etched in my mind, so perfect and permanent. My face burns with the memory of her body, and I try to shake it from my head on each breath.

I didn't go with Amy because:

~~Poncho's art is big and real.~~

SPRING[3]

Dolores doesn't come back the next week or the next. I'm glad because I don't have a sketch for her. I'm having second thoughts about the whole thing and hoping she's forgotten. I'm wondering if I could even do it, what it would mean if I could.

Then, one day, Dolores is at the door.

I'm inking a heart around a surgical scar, knotting the curves over skin twists—beautiful and grotesque. The client is middle aged and confident, happy with my work.

Dolores waits in the main room until the client has paid up and left. Then she's in front of me. She's dressed, but I'm imagining that snake and those flowers, Poncho's work, through her clothes.

"I can't copy Poncho," I tell her. "I'm not good enough."

Dolores puts her hand on my shoulder and squeezes. "Come on, Dubby. You have to do this for me."

I shrug, but not hard enough to knock her hand off.

"I knew I could count on you. Do you need to trace again?"

I don't, but she already has her shirt unbuttoned, so I take a better look at the whirlpool of peonies dripping to her navel, petals overlapping into feathers into scales. There's very little blank skin left—even the snake is hard

---

[3] But it doesn't feel like spring to Dubby. It's still cold, and what they call snow is slush, and what they call rain is icy pellets. It's the longest season, or maybe it only feels that way. There's hope. There's so much cruelty.

to find, eclipsed by later art.

I'll do this thing for Dolores and for me, too. I ought to know the truth.

Later, at the pool, I draw a straight line in the water, drilling with one hand, then the other. Breathe every five. Punch—hnhh. Punch. Punch. Punch. Punch. Punch—hnhh. Punch. Punch. The laps are like a mobius strip, when I flip at one end, then the other. The water is always the same.

Years ago, after we got Poncho tattoo-certified and set up our shop, he wanted me to take a drawing class, so I did. I used the last of my money, what I'd saved to move to California with Amy. I was blown away by that art class, by all that I'd never thought of—about perspective and the way people are proportioned. But a lot of it I'd already figured out on my own. The nuances of skin work, drawing over creases, veins, bones, wrinkles, the instructor didn't cover at all. She didn't know anything about tattoos. She said I lacked confidence, said I used the eraser too much. So I erased my whole sketch book, line by line, rubbed holes in the paper, and started over.

Back then, I still thought I could be an artist. Not just a sidekick. Not just the one who cleans the equipment, who drills Poncho's designs, right out of the book. So even when I'm done, it's not my work, everlasting on cold skin. It's still Poncho's. But it's the closest I can get.

I didn't go with Amy because:
~~Sex isn't eternal either.~~

*

The next day, I sit down with my tracing of Dolores's bird.

It's not a bad tattoo. The lines are clean. The shading is subtle. In fact, I feel bad covering it up. But it would never pass for Poncho. Dolores is right about that.

I can tell a few things about the artist from the work. Right-handed, that's easy. And older, I think, than Dolores or Poncho or me. Also, there's a firmness to the lines, a slant that defies what the bird is, that complicates it. An artist puts so much of themself into a tattoo.

Amy's hair was the lightest blond imaginable. Some nights, she'd let me color her hair with washable markers. I'd make rivers of blue and green and purple. Then, my hands tangled in that hair, looping the strands into intricate designs, the colors rubbing off on my fingers. She'd wash the color out in the morning. And I'd take her blotched pillowcase to the laundromat, disappointed to pull it from the dryer fresh and white again.

We picked California because it was far away and we could swim in the ocean and have summer all the time. She had only been there once, some hostel in Los Angeles. I'd never been but shared her dream. From movies, I suppose, or the way her voice softened when she talked about it. We were young and so romantic. Back then, I thought we could last.

I have to focus on this bird, on making it Poncho's. It's the colors and the lines. Poncho would thread Green 854 behind this line, but not that one. Poncho would balance the bird on Dolores's chest with a fish on her toe. Not every client would let him do it—few, in fact—but I know Poncho would ask, plead, beg, give discounts. This is where I can't copy Poncho. I don't have the nerve to ask Dolores for another piece of her skin. So the project is hopeless. He'll know right away. Still, this drawing, I'll make it good. The bird's face is so important. The eyes need irony, but the beak can't smirk, not even a little bit. I want to shade Blue 57, but Poncho wouldn't. Poncho would feather in Purple 628 or maybe 624.

Poncho still sells his paintings sometimes, or tries to. But mostly he stores them in his grandma's basement or in the shed at my parents' house. Except for some that he gives to random people who admire them. He's never given any to me. I've never tried to tell him how much I like them.

I couldn't tell you what his paintings are of, just that I like looking at them. The colors pull me into them, like I'm swimming in the shapes, holding my breath from one feeling to the next. Sometimes I find people I know inside them. Sometimes I find myself. But I'm never sure it's really me, and I don't ask.

I always wanted to be an artist, but I'm not. Just a tradesperson. Or maybe it's a craft, what I do. It's good that I get to work with Poncho, my best friend and business partner, because he's the real thing, and I want to be close to that.

I draw the fish anyway. Just in my sketchbook. I guess I'm drawing it for fun. I do have fun with it. The first lines come quickly and are perfect, but then my hands move more slowly. It starts out Poncho's but then it turns into mine. It starts as a favor to Dolores and a way to learn the truth, but now I can't let my fish down. My charming little fish.

When I swim and I have a design half-done, sometimes it will finish in my mind. I'll see it behind the 1-2-3-4-5, rippling on the bottom of the pool, flipping with my feet, splashing out of the water on the turn, just in front of my fingers on each pull. It will come together slowly, shimmering, and then it'll goddamn solidify. When it's clear in my mind, I hold it there for another hundred meters or so, let it set. Then I can climb out of the pool, shake the picture from my head, and try not to think about it as I take my shower. When I next get out my sketchbook, it's already in my fingers. I just tap my pencil, and it pours onto the page.

If not the art, floating behind my splashes, it's Amy.

I didn't go with Amy because:

~~I still have Poncho.~~

It's Tuesday afternoon again, and Dolores is sprawled on the workspace, her breasts bubbling out either side of a bra that can't quite hold them. She's so relaxed, talking as I drill tiny hole after tiny hole. "This guy, he's just my friend. I tell you I don't know what I was thinking, letting him work on me. I just got carried away. And then I was still mad at Poncho over that thing last fall, you know, the girl and the red turtle? *My* turtle? So I just did it. And then, you know, as soon as it was done—before the blood dried—I was sorry."

Her blood, it's thin like air, rubs right back into her skin in places. It's not like water at all. I blot it away as I work. It blurs the lines or darkens them, depending.

"I live in Cleveland, you know? Well, sort of outside. I've been there since right after high school. Can you believe that? But I come home all the time. I'm always in here, right? It's like a four-hour drive. My sister and niece live here. Sometimes my niece comes to stay with me, too. Sherry drives her out when things get too intense."

Whenever Dolores pauses, I nod. If she ends on a question, I grunt. I'm concentrating on her skin, the heat and the vibration of it. I can make the bird quiver with the same motion.

"Well, Sherry, my sister? Do you know her? She's having trouble with Hadyn now. She's fifteen and fucking feisty. And I'm laid off. No prospects for at least a month and probably longer. So I just drove out. I might even look for work around here. Hospitals everywhere, right? I do medical coding, have I told you that?"

"Mm."

"Yeah, it's this tattoo guy in Cleveland, outside of Cleveland, did this, I don't know what I was thinking." Whatever it was, she's thinking it again.

The feathers are turning out nicely. They look soft, yet alert. It's all in the angles.

"Anyway, I'm home for a stretch now and I'm terrified of running into Poncho before we get this damn bird fixed and healed. I'll be helping Sherry talk some sense into my niece, I hope. Not that anybody can do that. She's fifteen, you know?"

Dolores smiles, thinking about fifteen, then frowns like she's remembered something bad.

"My niece just doesn't realize. This shit will last the rest of her life. She gets all fucked up on some guy or some drug or some crime. Shit. She's just a kid and doesn't think. I can totally see her in some fucking knife fight or something, all cut up with scars or arrested. I'm afraid to even talk to her. I mean you can recover from that stuff, but not completely, you never completely get away from it."

She's waiting, so I have to speak. "Permanent record, right?"

"Yeah, look at my sister. I love her, but she's a mess. And that's coming from me, right?" She twists her arm, letting the vines, the frogs, and the starry night sparkle.

I could watch her arm forever, but she's blocking her chest, and time is running out. I remind her to be still.

"Sorry." She lowers her arm, and I dive in again. "How long until Poncho comes?"

There's a shuffle then, and the door starts to open. I gasp. Dolores grabs for her shirt. Blood spins like a thread from the bird to her waist as she hops off the table.

It's not Poncho, thank god, just a client. But it's time for Dolores to go. She blots at her skin and then gives up and puts her shirt on, holding it away from her chest so it won't stick. "I'll see you next week," she says, and she runs out the door. I'm alone with the cleanup, still seeing the bird, still feeling the buzz of the tattoo machine in my hand.

What Poncho has with Dolores, I don't understand it, but it's lasted long enough that I know it means something to them both. So part of me, at least, hopes this will work.

I'm not always sure I did the right thing, setting Poncho up here, getting him to tattoo. I mean, he's so good. He ought to spend all his time painting pictures, making art that'll last. These tattoo masterpieces of his—they're all doomed. They live only as long as the carrier—and sometimes not that long. You can protect paintings from knives and fires and acid. But people don't protect their own skin.

After work, I'm at the pool again. I flip water in a circle. It splashes up and under and marks me in the pool.

Sometimes words float behind my eyes, like the pictures. Whole sentences hover at the waterline, but I don't believe them.

I didn't go with Amy because:
~~I wanted to draw.~~

I'm at the tattoo shop late to meet Dolores, and it's eerie all alone. The metal equipment gleams, reflects in the windows, flashes the streetlights back out.

Dolores taps at the window, and I let her in. She smells like tequila and is in a quiet mood. I know how to sit with that. It's what I'm good at. She lies down on the table, and I start right away.

The bird is still, as motionless as Dolores underneath my fingertips and the palms of my hands. How does she make it so even her heart doesn't beat? Mine beats so hard. The bird is tense, gearing up for flight but not taking off, not yet. I color carefully, content to be quiet with her.

Eventually, I prick the last dot of orange 326, and a drop bubbles back. I blot it away and straighten. "Finished." She breathes deeply, and it sends each feather into its own individual quiver. Then she rises up, slowly and smoothly.

I hand her the mirror, and she studies the bird, her lips twisting at the corners. "I love it. It's just like Poncho." She hops off the table. "There's another thing, Dubby." She bites her lip in a way to suggest hesitance, but I think it's for show. "Poncho never does just one place at a time."

I pull the fish from my folder. It's like a koi, but different, evolved, and moving so fast in its stillness. "Do you have a good toe spot?" Dolores drops a shoe and then peels off a sock. Her foot is small and white, with only a few coils of ink that wrap underneath the arch.

We're both high on the tattoos and want to keep going.

Dolores watches the lines go down as my hands draw them. She's entranced like I am, inside the emerging fish. It's growing over muscle, will shift as she walks, roll with each step.

"Hey, Dubby." She speaks, finally, but she's still watching. The fish is surfacing. "Whatever happened to that friend of yours? Amy, was it? Is she still around?"

I focus on the tattoo machine, which suddenly feels nothing like a pencil. "She moved away." Needle in. Needle out. So fast, but so careful. I keep my attention on the zig and the zag of tiny scales.

"She was nice," Dolores says.

My eyes are fuzzy, but maybe it's blood that blurs the lines I'm drawing. Thinking of Amy, I have to step back. I used to stare at Amy's freckles until my eyes lost focus and the tiny dots formed floating castles with turrets and dolphins leaping over waves.

I only ever did one tattoo on Amy, my own initials, small but solid. She was sprinkled with freckles that I needled between. Amy couldn't sit still for more than those tiny letters, tense muscles, always fidgety. Her fingers wandered over my neck and arms as I worked.

I blot the blood from Dolores's skin, then I'm back in with the gun. The ghost fish, the clean outline, is looking pretty good, but there's still a ways to go. Blood lines weave in and out, swirl to Dolores's heel, and hang right at the edge of it.

It's like swimming now with my graceful fish, wavering through the water in my eyes. I keep tattooing, but I think about the rhythms in the pool, arms reaching, splashing, breathing every five.

It's finished. Dolores is glowing. "I'm glad the fish is the one I get to look at." She curls her toe, then stretches it out, then points it ballerina style. Then she pulls at my shoulder. I stand firm, but she curls herself toward me, almost falling off the table. She grabs hold of my arm as she hops to her feet. "You're a sweetheart, Dubby."

Rain is just starting when Dolores leaves. I try to think if there's an umbrella anywhere, but she's already sprinting to her car, holding her purse over her head as she dodges traffic.

I take every tattoo seriously. I don't care if it's a butterfly straight out of the book or some made-up Chinese character on a frat boy who doesn't even ask what it means. Because the frat boy might grow out of being an asshole, but he won't grow out of my tattoo. It will stretch with his belly, flap over his belt, fade in the sun— but it will still be his tattoo.

I disinfect the equipment and drop the cash in the safe. By the time I'm done, the rain comes down heavy like tiny needles. I don't have a raincoat, and the drops prick at my neck when I walk the two blocks to my car. I'm drenched by the time I get there and dripping as I drive to the pool. It's late, so I'm speeding, desperate to get a few laps in before the Y closes.

When I swim, I hold my favorite images in the front part of my head. Beautiful Amy, sunrise hair in my fingers. Silly Amy, stomping around in my rain boots. Sweet Amy, leaning into me. Holding my breath from color to color, from shape to shape, from feeling to feeling.

I didn't go with Amy because:
~~I made a mistake.~~

SUMMER[4]

Five years ago, the day before she left, Amy came to the tattoo shop. I was on my knees, scrubbing the floor. I stood and let the water drip from my rubber gloves.

I showed her around, my very own studio, the closed door to Poncho's room where he was setting up, the used couch, the brand new tattoo machine.

"You're sure about this," Amy said. Her freckles shimmered, but I managed not to touch them.

I breathed in deeply then counted to five as I let it out. "The money's spent."

"Our money."

"My half."

"I don't even care." This was the first time her voice sounded desperate. "You could still come with me."

We'd been through this. "I don't think so—could you promise me?"

"Maybe." The end of her ponytail twitched.

"I need to know it will last."

"Like Poncho's boring art." Amy said this loudly, then looked over her shoulder at Poncho's door.

I took another breath and held it. I floated through air and water.

Amy's eyes were red. Her hands were clenched fists, and her hair gave off tiny vibrations. "Fuck, Dubby. Five years. Five years we've been planning this."

"I'm sorry."

---

[4] Nobody is thinking about the weather. This section is five years ago and also right now.

Poncho burst from his studio then. His breath came evenly, but in puffs, and the corners of his mouth were springy. His arms hung, muscled but still. It was clear he'd been painting. "Let's do a mural out here, too," Poncho said. I considered the wide white wall, and Amy slipped behind me out the door.

Dolores has been gone since we did the fish, healing, I suppose. But one summer day, I'm in the shop, doing inventory of the ink colors, and there she is, falling out of a sundress and hugging me all at once.

On Dolores's thigh, there's a woodcutter. He has an axe raised up, poised to take a chunk out of something. She says, "I saw Poncho last night. I ran into him at Curly's, and everything is fine."

"Oh." It's like I missed my last breath before the turn, and now I'm going hard into the wall, screaming for air.

"He saw everything, but he didn't even notice the bird. We did it!" Dolores gives a little hop. The bird on her chest twitters.

I sit down at my desk. I didn't want Poncho to be mad, not at Dolores, or to be sad or hurt. But how could he not notice? It can't be real if he doesn't remember. It can't last if it isn't real.

"And the fish, Dubby. Guess what he said about the fish!" The vines on her arms are swelling and falling like ocean waves. I need to look away.

"What?"

"He said, 'Who did that pretty little fish?' He noticed

it was new and didn't even care. He traced it with his thumb. I didn't tell him it was you, because, well.... Should I tell him it was you?"

"Whatever you want." There's no reason left to care.

"Then I'll tell him. We're going to do the rest of my leg tonight." Dolores rubs an empty spot on her knee between a black web and a faded spider. There's water in my eyes again, so I find the fish, that fish, my fish, gearing to leap over the strap of her sandal.

"Can you wait for him?" I stand up sharply, sling my bag over my shoulder. "I have to go. Could you watch the place?"

"Sure." She's sitting on the desk now, her butt tearing a page from the open appointment book, legs swinging. "No appointments?"

"None."

I have to get to the pool. I have to pour myself into the water.

I can't swim in Poncho's paintings anymore.

When I swim, I will hold my favorite images in the front part of my head. Beautiful Amy, sunrise hair in my fingers. Silly Amy, stomping around in my rain boots. Sweet Amy, leaning into me. Those memories don't change—just their meaning.

And then there's that fish, ever-streaming-ever-rippling, as close as I can get to real. Maybe I can think of that fish, perfect, on Dolores's toe.

The Vortex

Joseph was concerned about the in/out doors at the restaurant where he worked. The doors were side by side and strictly enforced. They opened in opposite directions and shut much too quickly. He'd bussed tables in restaurants with in/out doors before, but none had created such a tight vortex.

Perhaps he was not worried enough.

Joseph continued to work his shift. He needed the money, and several of his coworkers were very pretty.

Allison was the bartender that day. She was an ordinary sort of person, though she didn't think so. She thought she was artistic in an unnamable way and possibly destined for greatness. She didn't expect to write a beautiful poem or paint a beautiful picture but suspected she might inspire a poem or painting or perhaps a legendary heroic act which would be remembered for all time. She didn't expect to perform the act, but for it to be performed in her honor or perhaps her defense.

She only needed to find the artist or hero. Not the skinny busser who had a crush on her. He might try but wouldn't be able to pull it off. Or the dishwashers and cooks who never talked to her unless she messed up an order or broke something. Her bar regulars? Not likely. A dowdy scientist and the rest deadbeats or office drones.

Allison was wrong about Joseph. He *was* a hero. He made a special effort to walk the wrong way through the in/out doors. To do so, he waited for another employee to burst through, caught the door before it swung shut, and slipped through swiftly to avoid being scolded or smashing into a waiter. Then he repeated the process for the other door.

Each time, he swung his arms wide. He walked against the whirlpool forces, scooping with his hands to push the airflow in the opposite direction and unwind the twisting energy. Joseph couldn't hope for much with these tactics. The vortex had been building strength for a long time, and he was just one man bussing tables on a weekday lunch shift.

The flow of movement in one door and out of a door directly adjacent creates a vortex of energy. And, as nearly everyone knows, vortexes, especially those made of energy, have a tendency to open portals to other dimensions.

Just think of the earth spinning always in the same direction. The vortex has created time, a dimension otherwise unknown. This may seem confusing, but scientists have it mostly in hand. Of course, we, in the "real world," are used to time and have incorporated it into our lives.

The dimension opened by the vortex at the restaurant would not be so easily incorporated. And despite Joseph's efforts, the portal had just emerged.

Twice that day, carrying plates to the kitchen—where *was* that busser?—Allison caught a flash of light. She searched the ceiling and walls for the source of it. Perhaps a drop of water spinning off the metal surface of the "in" door. She found no wet spot, no leak. But Allison was not a plumber—she was a bartender! She didn't tell anyone.

On the other side of the vortex, through the gradually opening portal to another dimension, Grolf toiled in the dish pit. Bins of silver. Square plates, round plates, dimple bowls, ramekins. He scraped. He racked. He pushed the greasy shapes into the mouth of the dish machine. Hot water spewed between plastic curtains. It speckled Grolf's face with grime and soap and sweat. Grolf had no time to worry about the portal. He had no time to worry if another dimension would be worse than time.

Time, for what it's worth, was the fourth dimension in the world most commonly called "reality." The first dimension by the same count was unlivable unless you were a speck smaller than you could make with a pencil, a speck so small that you had no size but were made up entirely of abstract thought. The fourth dimension made all things livable, even death. The fourth dimension was the worst thing that had ever happened to those living in the world called "reality."

Grolf didn't know anything about the world called "reality," but, if pressed, he might have argued that there was some degree of "realness" to his own world. In Grolf's unnamed world, "time" was numbered "ninth" by physicists, though Grolf did not know it.

However, Grolf knew time, knew the tragedy that time inflicted. It meant that when he washed dishes he could not also be with his wife and newborn quintuplets. Time separated the things Grolf did so that the enjoyable things sat apart from those which were necessity.

On this day, Grolf thought about something worse. All of it would end. Grolf, his new wife, all five of his even newer quintuplets. Time granted death to beings who had only just achieved life—Grolf couldn't bear the injustice.

For his part, Joseph didn't think about time as a dimension, certainly not one enabled by a vortex similar to the in/out doors. Instead, time was something he could trade for money or fun or knowledge. Joseph was short on time because he worked two jobs and took classes at the community college. He also got roped into babysitting his sister's kids because he lived above her garage. When he feared the vortex created by the in/out doors, Joseph thought about what frightening things might exist beyond the portal. Monsters, perhaps, or maybe an even more grossly exploitative economic system. Time was not the dimension that concerned him.

Allison? She hated time. And loved it too. She loved the time far in the future she hadn't yet reached, even while she hated the time directly in front of her. Surely she'd be granted fame and glory, somehow, even though the headshots she'd just spent a bundle on made her eyes look kind of glazed and lifeless.

Dr. Pluton was perplexed by these various notions of time and dimension. She didn't understand how a dimension could be shared and somehow within and without two other dimensions, one labeled "reality" and one unlabeled. She didn't understand how time could be a dimension and some speck of abstract space and how it also could be a tragedy and a commodity and whatever thing it became in Allison's thinking. Dr. Pluton needed more time—oh!—to figure it out, but she wouldn't get that time. She needed another drink, too—where was that bartender? She put her hands to her head and massaged her temples.

Joseph unwound another wrapping of the vortex, carefully timing the swing of the doors and spreading his arms wide. Allison blinked her eyes in rapid succession trying to see the water drop, trying not to see it. On the other side, Grolf ignored the portal, even as it widened, gaping through the splash of the dishwashing machine.

Dr. Pluton stood aside from events just like she distanced herself from the other bar regulars. As a physicist, she knew that time, the fourth/ninth dimension, would march them toward the full opening of the portal and the clashing of "reality" with another world that was not it. But she had a good idea, or perhaps an unsubstantiated hope, that for the next ten minutes all parties were safe, and the bartender could mix her another old fashioned. When those ten minutes were up, Dr. Pluton would know more about clashing realities than even she wanted to. But for the moment, three drinks deep, Dr. Pluton couldn't explain any of it.

Final Journal Entry of
Dr. Francis Longfellow Hendrix,
Lead Scientist at Laboratory 78
Edited by A. L. White

Ghosts don't "float" or "hover." Instead, they have to swim through air. Tests prove they are hardly more substantial than air and suggest the reason for such a system of locomotion. But ghosts *are* more substantial than air. Otherwise, they'd dissipate. And that was the thought that started it all. (Nostalgia abounds.)

My research is drawing to a close. Citing "failure to produce practical application," they[1] are shutting me down. Thus, I must make sense of a mere six years' worth of findings.

Ghosts, then, are more substantial than air. Otherwise

---

1 Editor's note: Hendrix refers to the FCCPN, which provided the bulk of the laboratory's funding.

they would dissipate, which is what non-ghost souls do. Their particles scatter through atmosphere. The ghost holds together its substance through strong emotion. The emotion is most often rage but can also be another robust emotion such as love or jealousy or grief.

Think about an emotion that can overcome intense pain—you'll see it's usually rage and thus why most ghosts are angry. It's that rage we should fear, not the ghostliness. (But what mortal ever understood enough to fear the right things?)[2]

The strong emotion is identical to the one felt by the donor specimen at the moment of death which appears to be due to the clear need for continuity. If a soul releases its binding emotion, its particles dissipate.[3] Typically, dissipation occurs at 2.36 seconds, though the process can be slowed as much as 15% by temperatures below -7° C. Discovery of the "slowing principal" led to experiments

---

2 Editor's note: Other editors have redacted this sentence, as it appears to be speculative in nature, an unscientific digression. Although the topic corresponds to the doctor's interests and proclivities, there have been found no notes, either private or published, to indicate that Hendrix ever launched a formal study of the justification of fears of human beings.

3 Editor's note: Hendrix does not directly address the cause of dissipation in these notes, but we can assume it was on his mind. See his published writings on the theory of pain as dissipating factor, a controversial opinion at the time. Renowned physicist Alice Pregnor, as well as paranormal chemists Eckert, Proust, and Mendez disputed pain's influence, claiming death alone as primary force of dissipation. Hawkins and Wang's study to procure and quantify painless death was funded the next year, perhaps inspired by the spat. Though fascinating in its process, the experiment was ultimately inconclusive.

meant to stop or reverse dissipation. Lab assistant T-4 led the team with no reported success.

Limited length of experimental opportunity precludes speculation about the longevity of ghosts. Thirty-six of our current specimens have been with us since the beginning. Thus, we can reasonably hypothesize, though not conclude, a life expectancy (or death expectancy—haha!) greater than six years.

More recent experiments have aimed at further extrapolation of age with a process dubbed "particle decay." While many ghosts uphold their emotion for years, their "bonding principle" may flag with time, so that a subset of the outer particles breaks free into the surrounding non-ghost particles: The ghost seems to "shrink." Under ordinary circumstances, the lost particles are unable to re-bond, even if the ghost should experience a surge in emotion (the occurrence is rare). In its natural habitat, the ghost will be unable to enlarge itself by accumulating or re-accumulating floating particles because of the failure of those particles to bond.

Lab experiments have yet to successfully bond ghost particles with non-ghost particles or ghost particles from two or more originating sources (i.e. souls). Shutdown of facilities eliminates reasonable hope of successful bonding in the future.

In the lab, however, we *have* managed to recreate, under highly controlled circumstances, the re-connection of particles of the same source, which have been disconnected but not lost. The new connections, however, are tenuous. Subject-ghost does not retain reallocated particles for long. Average holding time is 43 minutes. The longest recorded holding was 157 minutes.

Speculation forward—or predicting when the ghost will decay past solvency—has been inconclusive. However, by studying the rate of decay in individual ghosts, estimating death mass, and extrapolating backwards, we can date a ghost with a theorized 97% accuracy. It's important to note that decay rates vary from specimen to specimen and by season and environment.

Does the ghost mind the loss of its particles? This is an interesting question, though difficult to determine in the lab setting through scientific procedure. Subjects do not *seem* to notice. That is, there is no measurable deviation in the recorded emanations beyond the decrease of the original emotion, which is hypothesized as the cause of the lessening of the ghost-self in the first place.

Assistant T-6 has speculated that the loss of particles may cause the lessening of emotive emanations, rather than the reverse. The theory is interesting, but at this time untestable.

Rage, as has been mentioned, is the most common emotional adhesive, followed by love, jealousy, and melancholy. Other feelings with documented ghost presences are fear, anxiety, and surprise.

Surprise is a new finding. While I have long suspected its possibility, I have only recently managed to obtain proof, the obstacle being the fleeting nature of surprise. No ghost can last longer than its binding emotion.

Instruments of particular sensitivity are thus required to detect the ghost before dissipation destroys the specimen. There has also been the challenge of procuring surprise as a last-felt emotion for the test subject. The preparation of measuring devices and setting of the experiment often eliminate the "element" of surprise. Therefore, to procure a true surprise, it's been necessary to conduct experiments in the field, where the situation is less controllable and the measurements less precise. Despite these obstacles, we've had encouraging results thus far. At the time of the field experiments, all permits[4] were, obviously, in order.

Though funding has been cut, and the laboratory is shutting down, effective immediately, this scientist finds it productive and/or nostalgic to contemplate the original goals of the project.[5]

Practical Application: Obtainment of ghosthood rather than dissipation upon predictable death. At time of

---

4 Editor's note: Hendrix here references the infamous "lost permits." The papers themselves have never surfaced, and historians speculate about not only their content and legality but their very existence. Note, however, the casual confidence with which Hendrix mentions them. This editor is content that Hendrix believed he had permission for whatever grotesqueries were performed. The question of whether those permissions included "surprising subjects to death," and whether those surprises occurred in the laboratory or in the field, may never be answered, though it is certainly intriguing and has prompted numerous investigations.

5 Editor's note: Hendrix seems, at this point, to be "starting over." Certain biographers have speculated that an interruption may have occurred during this point in his reflections. Martin et al. goes so far as to hypothesize that a mysterious "other" lured him, momentarily, away. This editor merely deems it necessary to note that the lack of organization is not characteristic of the doctor and should undoubtedly be attributed to the stressful nature of the shutdown.

funding cut, the initiative was an estimated 62% to goal.

Practical application: Containing "loved ones" in situations of predictable death. As above, 62%.

Practical application: Re-constituting dissipated "loved ones" in cases of unpredicted death. 0% progress.

Practical application: Ghosts as pets? Experimentation not begun. 0% progress prior to shut down. [6]

As rendered in lore, ghosts (or un-dissipated soul particles) can pass through walls comprised of drywall, insulation, steel, aluminum, and most varieties of wood, cardboard, plaster, etc., without dissipation.

Some materials prove more troublesome to the ghost. (Thus most useful to the scientist.)

Hypothesis formed at observation of ghosts passing through walls but avoiding windows. Series of tests: Forcing particle clumps (ghosts) through sheets of glass. An average of 7.8% of particles dissipated upon each pass-through.

This scientist is observing nostalgia at recording of first breakthrough regarding the "non-break-through" material.

Support teams led experiments on other glass-like substances. The most successful substance for trapping soul particles, thus far, is water.

Let me be clear: A ghost can pass through water, but not without 100% dissipation. Effectively, then, the only

---

[6] Editor's note: Scholars debate continuity at this point. Martin et al. go so far as to posit another interruption.

escape through water is suicide, which ghosts, in most cases, have seemed averse to. There has been only one recorded incident. Research into the motive for that case has been inconclusive.

Laboratory 78 built a series of cages that are best imagined as inverse aquariums. Walls, floor, and ceiling are constructed of parallel sheets of glass with distilled water encased between the sheets.

After losing specimen 5 to probable self-extermination, we increased surveillance on the remaining 117 specimens under study.

Specimen 6, positioned adjacent to 5, exhibited odd behaviors, including crashing against the glass. It averaged four bumps per hour for a span of 73 hours. No collision was forceful enough to propel the ghost through the glass and thus dissipate.

I should here note that one of the lab assistants (T-14) has an unsettling habit of calling the specimen by the first name of its source organism. This one he called "Frederick," subsequently shortened to "Fred." After the "frenzy" started, the entire team began to call it "Fredzy."

At the end of Fredzy's tantrum, the specimen recorded a 28.73% decrease in mass. Water in the walls of the cage showed a previously undetected cloudiness. Eager to analyze the contained water, we drained the cage and found the non-water substance to be a solution of 78% nitrogen, 12% helium and 4.5% beryllium. The remaining 5.5% was an unidentifiable substance that certain lab assistants playfully called "ghostium."

Unluckily, the specimen was lost to dissipation during the transfer.

Several of the lab assistants, including T-3, T-11, and T-14, speculate that Fredzy did not dissipate but "escaped." We senior scientists discourage idle gossip, but some talk is to be expected.

The first cages of the anti-aquarium design had a 1-cm water thickness between double 1-cm glass walls, which tended to distort the appearance of the already transparent particle entities. I've since experimented with thinner water walls. Current boxes have .03-cm water thickness and still hold 98% of the particles while providing 375% improvement in visibility.

Visibility being problematic, the color division, led by assistant T-7, has attempted to enhance the specimen with vapor dies. No reported success.

Apart from aquox[7] labeling and provenance, there is no conclusive method of identification of soul particles. However, emotional readout can serve as a speculative "fingerprint" that is 85% accurate.[8]

A rogue specimen arrived yesterday. I admittedly acted counter to current protocols and am hesitant to report on it. But what, after all, have I left to lose?

---

[7] Editor's Note: The term "aquox" was laboratory jargon for the "reverse aquariums," in which specimen were contained and studied.

[8] Editor's Note: Many scholars have noted a change in ink color at this point in the original document. After this sentence, the words are a brighter shade of blue.

It brought immediate memories of the old days. A time of the crudest instruments, the barest records. Necessarily, it was a time of 0% record/biography of the deceased/donating organisms. Nostalgia (measured at 65% nitrogen, 14% helium, 4.5% beryllium and the rest indecipherable) surged.

And of course I would have turned this one away had funding not been cut. Had not the dissipation of the lab been imminent, and had not nostalgia (+/- 14% helium) been heaving in the atmosphere. I should have locked the loading docks. Dozens of rogue specimens appear each month—brought by scavengers, mothers, soldiers—I sniff, then refuse. With current regulations, we all do.

And funds. No more barrel scraping. Then no funds at all. And no more sniffing. The laboratory dissipates, even as I jot down these anxious notes.

I am alone here, in the lab. The instruments are boxed. Only my desk lamp glows into the surrounding darkness.

But there was something about this one. When I sniffed the case, I detected an unusual quality, an odor that defied identification. And so I paid the pittance this boyfriend asked and dropped the specimen into a vacant aquox.

I'm rushed. Dissipation looms. Thus, these notes are scattered, unprofessional. I long for the old days.

The careful, painstaking details.

The science.

Onward.

Similarities of the ghost to the deceased, of particle mass to donor organism: Few observed. Even fewer measurable. Ghosts retain less than 0.056% of gender, appearance, memory, personality.

Lab assistant T-11 doubted. Maintained and sought to test hypothesis that certain personality traits remained. I admit skepticism that she could devise a method to test the theory. After four months, her funding has been cut with the rest of ours. Inconclusive.

Lab assistant T-45 insists on exploring "the lore," as he persists in calling it. However, attempts to determine link between corpse and spirit are inconclusive. In the turmoil of the shutdown, as a "last ditch" effort, I discovered T-45 attempting the "stake in the heart" method. Minimal scolding. Results, of course, inconclusive.

Important to note for probable lay readers of scientific journal: Corpse is not equal to donor organism. A triangle, in effect, is established between ghost (non-dissipated soul particles), original living organism (person), and corpse (de-animated body). Relationship theories abound. 37% progress toward understanding of relationship between the three.

Laboratory 85% shut down. Anti-aquariums (aquox) 12% dissembled. Instruments 56% returned to donors. De-animated bodies 27% returned to donor families.

My fingers are so knobbly. Knuckles larger than the phalanges connecting them. And curled almost, twisted like the roots of a tree.

How have I not noticed it before?[9]

The lights are soft green in the specimen room. It seems to be an effect of the reflecting water inside the glass sheets. Bouncing from transparent wall to wall to wall. But it can't be that, and we all know it. At least the senior fellows do. I must assume so, with their powers of observation so honed.

We don't talk about it. Any of us.[10]

Of course, early on, I ran some tests.

And I caught T-7 here[11] once. T-5. T-8. Of course T-14 and T-15. Different nights, different instruments, held low or nestled in the folds of the lab coat.

On the security footage, they hide until the doors are locked. Tiptoe to the room, eyes agleam. Each with a

---

[9] Editor's note: Some (including Higgins, Malter and Gray, and DeJulio et al.) cite this odd passage on "knobbly" hands as evidence of mental deterioration and/or a psychic slip. Others insist on a literary rationale for the passage. Hawkins notes a metaphoric resonance, aligning the knuckles with the ghosts and phalanges with "loved ones." This editor declines to enter the debate, yet cannot resist pointing out that Hendrix did have long, thin fingers with thick, protroding knuckles. Let readers of the text draw their own conclusions.

[10] Editor's note: Corroboration of a lack of communication presents obvious challenges. DeJulio, et al. find Hendrix's claim credible. See Felix, Menst, and Honario for an argument discounting it.

[11] Editor's note: Hendrix seems to be writing this segment from inside the specimen room, though he earlier mentions the light from his desk (in an adjacent room), and the notes themselves were found on the desk. Gangnum and Peters speculate that he is merely imagining himself wandering the lab, while Simpson posits the existence of a subsequently lost clipboard.

different measuring device—some vial or wand or spectrometer. And then they measure, test, record. Record what? Nothing. Nothing. Later, they try to sneak out, tripping alarm wires. I get the call. I have to document the breach, but I'm careful never to ask, or let them confess, what they tried to measure. Not too worried they'll surprise me with explanations. Oh! the surprise.

T-11 didn't sneak out but slept on the floor. Blended into the morning crew with rumpled lab coat the only giveaway. And nothing for her notes but a frustrated squiggle.

We all sense what it is—but without the measurement, the proof, we don't even have words.

Full shutdown is in effect tomorrow. Yet facility is 14% operational overnight. This scientist intends to run another set of tests, realistically expecting little conclusive evidence. But, oh, what the hell?[12]

---

[12] Editor's note: Attempts to interpret the final line of the doctor's missive, and possibly the last words he ever wrote, have sparked wide-ranging debate. How does the allusion to "hell" tie in to the doctor's experiments with ghosts? His views of the afterlife? His frustration at having been shut down just six years into the study? Or do the words have a darker meaning relating to his disappearance? Were his notes hiding rather than illuminating the experiments he'd performed in his six years of occult study? Had the doctor found a "way to hell"? This editor finds such speculation to be unproductive at best and harmful at worst. Rumors of Hendrix's "ghost" have been dismissed by all but the most untrustworthy of the laboratory staff. Upon shutdown of the laboratories, notice of Hendrix's disappearance, and the subsequent finding of these last notes, investigators sealed the scene and deployed the most sensitive processes and instruments in combing the grounds. Neither ghost nor corpse nor living Hendrix has been found. Despite the "haunting" claims of loved ones and fans, Hennepin and Ruiz claim dissipation as the most likely scenario. Golder and Eames speculate

about a romantic entanglement with assistant T-11. Let readers of the text draw their own conclusions.

  To find a person, a closure, the man himself, or some scrap of note or bone…these projects start with that aspiration (unnamed) but end with nothing of the sort. Or do they? This editor found something—a shiver that moved through the shoulders and then dispersed. Was it bone tracing bone, catching on a knobbly knuckle, or something else? Except, of course, nothing. No equipment remained to date such a blast or to measure the energy. Was it held over from that year of disappearing or much later? Could it be a life run its natural course? That shiver. Said not with a whisper but with less than that, in words like an itch, like a tingle: "I found you." Let readers of the text draw their own conclusions.

Garden

I never had children, but over the years my garden became like one, and isn't it trite to say so? I cradle seedlings with soft earth, feed them water and sun and rotting vegetables until they are grown, and then, just like children, I chop off their heads and eat them. One crisp spring morning, I was preparing the beds: putting down fresh compost, churning it and loosening the soil until it was soft and pillowy. I stripped off my clothes and sat down in the bed. I shuffled my legs into the richness of it and felt a tingle and then an itch through all my buried skin. I moved my legs deeper and scooped handfuls of earth over the mountains of my knees, the slopes of my thighs, until I felt knives and needles through them. The veins wriggled beneath my skin. Then my skin peeled open in a hundred tiny places. There were bright splashes of red, and the veins surfaced, one by one, as long pink noodles. They tunneled out of my legs and wriggled into the soil. A soft rain began to fall. It smelled like heaven. I shuffled my legs deeper again, and earthworms rose up. The worms were the same color as my skin but more alive. They twisted with the veins so that no one could have told which was which—I couldn't, and certainly not you—and then hundreds of them nosed through the dirt until they found the holes in my legs, like mouths agape. They squirmed into the holes, and it felt like knives and needles, then like itching and then a tight tingle, almost like sex. I stood up from the bed and hosed off my legs and bandaged them. I stumbled from blood loss, from the certainty that I would feed them again. The tomatoes were rich that year and sweet. Their juice was thick and dark like blood.

Sleep Birds

The grass underneath us was un-mowed and puffy. I moved aside some small rocks and a stick, then the earth welcomed my body onto it. I settled, sunk. The baby was happy on her tummy and drooling, the milk from my body both sour and sweet in her breath. On the walk up the hill, she had clung to me, her legs tight around my hips and her fingers caught in my hair. But now I leaned back on my elbows and squinted not quite into the sun. We were alone as far as I could see, on top of the hill, though other picnics must have been spread near the bottom. The baby gurgled, and I rolled to my side, curled around her. I pulled my backpack beneath my head and, with one hand encircling the tight sausage of her thigh, I closed my eyes and let sleep come.

Slowly it dropped from the bright sky, darkened into black-red heaviness behind my eyelids. The weight on my chest of sleep descending was the weight of one bird, then another and another, landing, each so light. But as they stacked on top of each other, the bottom birds sank into my skin. Bird feet pierced my chest and belly and thighs. More landed, jostling the hooked ones, and bird toes drilled deeper. The sky was dark with sleep and with birds, their wings open, then closing. Toes and feathers tangled in my hair. The feathers pillowed me like the grass beneath, and I was sinking upward as the birds descended and kept descending.

Then the baby flinched. There was fresh flapping and the release of toes like hooks. My eyes opened to a shallow strip of my skin as the birds hopped briefly off me. Blood lifted with their feet and rivered into pools over my thighs and my shins, dividing and connecting. A pattern of red lace against my skin beneath it and then the birds again over my chest, over my stomach, over my legs. I couldn't see my hand, which held tight to the baby's thigh, except for a sliver that was still bird-free and where bulged a single vein. I caught just a glimpse of that vein between feathers, snaking and rolling with the tension in my hand. I willed my hand to relax so I wouldn't shake or scare the baby, keeping my fingers firm on baby thigh. Her face was to the ground, and she was maybe asleep or maybe not. And then one more bird landed square on the spot of back my hand and bulging vein. The bird landed there with its feet, and it leaned forward with its head, and then its beak levered down. Heavy with sleep and red-black darkness that shimmered from the bird's feathers, I saw and felt the bird pluck the vein from my hand like a worm that it had pulled from soft-tilled earth.

The vein, like a worm, fought and wriggled to hide in the skin of my hand, but the bird pulled it up, tossed its head into the air, and swallowed the vein in two gulps. Then it lifted and flapped and looked down at us. It signaled, somehow, to the other sleep birds to fly away, too.

And so I woke, hard, and the blood was red instead of black, and the hole in my hand was stark, and the pain felt bright. I had lost my grip on the baby's thigh, but she was still there, not carried off. Trailing from her mouth was a pink worm. Another? No. The vein from my hand after all. And then she slurped it. The tail end whipped as it broke free from my hand, smacked her on the nose before disappearing. It spattered blood flecks on her cheeks, and they looked like glitter.

Fishing

Her legs dangle off the end of the pier, toes dipping into the water unless she curls them up to skim the surface. When the hook lifts, fishless—wormless, too—three drops fall to the lake's surface. A circle, cut by another, cut by another.

The fish are far beneath and don't notice. It is dark and quiet at the bottom of the lake. But the hook drops, wormed again, and now the fish dart for it, attack it at angles, grazing the sharp part, missing the barb. The angle is luck that has turned into habit that has turned into longevity. They are big, these fish. So big they won't be suckered by the old worm-and-hook trick.

She dumps the last of her worms into the lake: a single lump of writhing pink skin, tubes that wrap into circles, concentric rings eating themselves and each other. The fish still hit the mass at oblique angles, the luck and the longevity too much of a habit now. The ball of worms hits the bottom of the lake where it sends up a cloud of muck and murkiness.

The hook is swinging, a circle, a pendulum from the end of the pole, propped over the tackle box. Her legs are bare in front of her, the ragged edge of her cutoffs not long enough to cover the pockets or any part of her thighs, really. Her legs are skinny, too.

When the fishhook stops swinging, she splashes it into the water, rubs the last of the worm guts against the short strip of denim until the hook is shiny again. Then she dips it, so carefully, into the skin of her thigh. The tip pierces the skin, and in goes the barb, too. She wriggles it, a tiny circle, then pushes it deeper until it catches. She pulls, slow so the vein she's snagged will stay intact. She pulls until it's worm-length, and then she stops. She pinches it loose with two fingernails and works it more securely onto the hook. She casts the line.

Three drops of blood spark the water beneath the pier, their misaligned concentric circles crashing. Farther out, the hook has hit the water with the vein, and the fish are wild for it. Big fish, lucky fish (old fish) drop the habit of the oblique angle and aim straight for the vein, the hook. A smear of greasy blood spreads over the surface of the lake as bubbles burst beneath it, pocking the skin in non-concentric circles.

Heads butt, open mouths clash around the sharp barb. The fish devour each other, crunching into bones that bite back. Tooth clutches tail until the loop is a worm, is a vein. It oozes blood, and it writhes.

The girl has dropped her fishing pole. She is bandaging her leg and laughing.

Roar

The first time I heard the train roar by our trailer, I was in the kitchen washing dishes with Goldie, the parakeet. The dishes rattled. Goldie's cage swung and knocked him off his perch. He flapped against the metal wires of the cage, and still the train howled. The trailer began to sway. The noise drowned out the talk radio my brother, Clay, had cranked to top volume in the next room. Clay took a single bound into the center of the kitchen. "What's with the bird?" I gripped the edge of the sink and leaned back, pretending that the grease stain on the ceiling was a crystal chandelier about shatter over us. I thought I heard children's screams blended with the train's voice and decided the apocalypse had come.

It turns out that was just the custom in the trailer park, though. All the kids outside would stop their games of freeze tag or kickball and yell as loud as they could every time the train barreled through.

I was not pregnant then, not pregnant at all it turned out. But I thought I was. In fact, I was thoroughly convinced of it. My never-to-be-born child had already triggered the fight that had cost me my boyfriend and led me to live in a doublewide with my brother. Any kid with that much influence must be real, you know?

Jeremy didn't leave me because I was pregnant. He just insisted that he couldn't be a father. He was all mystical about it. He said if he had a son or a daughter, even a microscopic speck of a son or a daughter, he would know. He would *feel* it somehow. And that led him to the conclusion that I must be cheating on him. Of course I wasn't.

Jeremy wasn't angry about the affair he decided I'd had. He just wanted to talk about what it meant about our relationship. He wondered, would my other lover feel comfortable getting coffee or maybe smoking with us sometime, so we could really get at this from every angle?

I wasn't in the mood. And being all hormonally amped up by my pregnancy, I told him just how I felt about him and his damn sensitivity. Then I left.

When I showed up at Clay's with two mismatched suitcases and the swinging bird cage, the first thing he said was, "Who cheated?"

As if it were ever that simple.

It didn't look like Clay was going to help me with my suitcases, but when I swung one out to him, he caught it gracefully. Clay is tall and very skinny, and it looked like the suitcase would throw him off balance, but once he had a hold of it, he stood up straight as if it weighed nothing. I told him no one had cheated, but it was complicated, and he wouldn't understand. It's hard to talk to Clay sometimes without confessing everything. He has a manipulative way about him that he must have learned in the seminary.

Clay leaned away from the birdcage. "You can stay here as long as you like."

He didn't even own the trailer. Our parents had left it to him.

I said that as if they died, didn't I? They didn't. They moved to Florida. First just for the winter, which is why they bought the trailer. But it didn't take long for them to abandon it to live in Florida year-round. So they didn't even leave it for Clay. They just left it for empty, and he moved in. They gave us both keys, but nobody expected either of us to live there.

This was all happening the fall after I graduated from college. So I had my teaching license but no job. I was a high school math teacher, but then I guess I wasn't yet.

I held up well in that first encounter with Clay, not saying a word about being knocked up. But it's not that impressive. I didn't make it through the first hour.

Clay got out this strong incense, like the kind they use in church on special occasions. He probably got it at the priest store. He had almost become a priest but then quit.

Then Clay kicked himself into the recliner and said, "Jen, that bird really stinks."

"She does not."

"Maybe it's you, then."

"Don't be an ass."

"So, really, why are you here?"

So you can see why I couldn't help blurting it out with that incense going up and him using his holy voice and all. "I'm pregnant, and we got in a fight about it, and now I don't know what to do."

"Holy shit." Clay clicked out of his priest voice. "What *are* you going to do?"

The Roar came with the trains, and the trains weren't regular, so the Roar wasn't either. I never knew when one would blast through and the children would scream. When I jumped, just a bit, I felt a solidness in my gut that I imagined to be the baby.

Jeremy's apartment was on the third floor of an old house that was cut up into chunks. I was always creeped out by this weird door that went to the attic. The door was locked, and we didn't have a key, so I never saw behind it. But what was to stop it from opening from the other side?

I was also scared of these guys that came by when we first moved in. They claimed they'd left something inside before we got there. I wasn't home at the time, but Jeremy just let them in to look around. I freaked out later when I heard the story. Even if they were telling the truth, it was no good. The something was probably a gun. Jeremy figured it was just weed. I was scared. Jeremy was not scared at all. He was very neighborly all the time.

Clay made a confession to me, too, that first evening I spent in the trailer: "So, Mom and Dad don't know I'm living here."

I was wadded into the papasan chair, and he was propped on the recliner. We each held a remote control, but neither of us made the first move to turn on the TV or radio.

"Why *are* you here?" I asked him.

"Don't tell them, okay?" Clay kicked one shoe off his foot, and it balanced on his toe before dropping to the carpet. Then he shoved off the other one.

"Fine, you don't tell them that I'm here either. Or that I'm—you know."

"I know."

Clay and I have always been pretty close in some ways, but it's not like we shared secrets. So this was kind of a big deal. We were just an ordinary family growing up, out of a sitcom maybe, watching TV at the dinner table. Except Clay liked God so much, and that confused me and our parents, too.

After a few weeks of moping, I decided I needed some income. It was the end of September by then and too late to apply for teaching jobs, so I thought working as a math tutor might be my best bet, and I made some flyers.

I drew straight lines with a pencil and wrote "Math Teacher For Hire" across the top in every color of the Crayola marker set. I put my name and number and that I had a degree and a license. I didn't name a fee because I thought I would negotiate. I drew little math symbols around the margins. Then I covered all of Rosedale Mobile Community with them—mostly telephone poles, trees, and all sides of the playground structure. I stuffed mailboxes until a man in a yellow bathrobe yelled at me.

Gloria Brough called the very next day for me to tutor her son Scott, who ended up being my only client, but a regular one. It turned out that Scott didn't need much tutoring, except maybe in the fashion department, but I didn't want to touch that. The kid wore a bowtie and carried a briefcase. We got along well, however, and his mom paid what I asked.

It's weird, I know, that I didn't just take a pregnancy test, because that's what people do, right? I couldn't bring myself to buy one.

My car only started about every third day, but since I didn't have anywhere to go, that wasn't much of a problem. I'd wander out to the driveway most days and turn the key a few times. If it started, I'd take off. There wasn't any place to walk except around the little trailer park. No stores or anything within about five miles.

Usually, when the car started, I'd drive to Walgreen's. I'd walk slowly down the pregnancy test aisle with the basket on my arm, looking right and left but never making eye contact with other customers or with the test itself. Once or twice I managed to stop in front of the tests and stare directly at them. I even read the front of the boxes. But I never got so far as to touch one. I would walk on and buy something else. Toilet paper, or aspirin, or tampons. Even when that girl from my high school, Maureen Bergoff, wasn't working, I couldn't do it. Twice, I drove to other pharmacies, in neighboring towns, but I didn't have any luck in those either.

One of the best things about having a cell phone, even the old kind before smart phones, is that your parents won't necessarily find out that you've moved out of your apartment and are staying without permission in their mobile home. I talked to my mom two or three times a week like always. The only issue was remembering not to let her hear Clay's voice in the background unless I could make up a reason that we would be hanging out together, which was not as easy as it sounds.

She asked about Jeremy sometimes, but I'd just say, "He's fine," and then we'd talk about something else.

"So you haven't found a teaching job yet?" she'd often ask.

"No, Mom. They don't hire mid-year."

"So you'll have to wait until next fall."

"Uh-huh."

Repeating things we both knew was her way of showing sympathy, and she also used a sympathetic voice. It was really annoying.

Sometimes I helped Scott with his homework after school, but other times he didn't have any or didn't need help. He was in third grade, so it was all easy, but I got bored sometimes and tried to teach him.

"Here, let me teach you some algebra," I said one time. Scott wasn't done with his real homework, but it was pretty pointless stuff, I could tell.

"Algebra? I'm not supposed to know algebra until like eighth grade." He was standing at the counter in the kitchen where he always did his homework.

"You're smart."

"Thanks." Scott twisted his mouth like he was suspicious. "Okay."

I wrote $4 + x = 7$ in his notebook. "So how much is x?"

"Hey, that's my Social Studies!"

I apologized, erased the equation, and rewrote it in his math notebook. "So how much is x?"

"What?"

"What number is x pretending to be?" I underlined the x twice, then tapped at it.

Scott put his head over the notebook on the kitchen counter and kicked a foot, softly, at the cabinet underneath. "3." He looked up. "That's not hard at all."

I wrote $x = 3$ in the notebook. "So x equals 3. That's it. That's algebra."

"x equals 3? That's algebra?"

"Yep." I was feeling pretty proud of myself. Math teacher me.

"I just have to remember that x equals 3?"

"No—"

"—You just said."

"x doesn't always.... It's different every time."

"Huh?"

"You have to figure out x. It's different every time."

"I don't get it."

I flipped my pencil on the table and watched it bounce. "Never mind."

So maybe Scott wasn't as smart as I thought, or maybe third graders aren't ready for x and y. You'd think I'd know, what with my degree and all, but it's hard to keep it straight—age and mental development and stuff.

Another thing you might want to know is that Goldie is not a parakeet. She's a canary. But I've always thought parakeets sounded interesting and that it might be fun to fool you. Maybe it would add something exotic to the story.

Jeremy's older sister came by later that week. She was kind of a weirdo but also really nice. Jeremy and I used to stay in her apartment when she traveled, and it had this tiny balcony we'd wedge ourselves onto, dangling our legs through the rail. Once my flip-flop fell off, and I never found it, even the next day when I searched the parking lot.

She brought a car seat and a stroller. Both were new and nice. Jeremy must not have told her about the kid's suspected parentage.

"This is too expensive," I said.

"Eh, whatever." She waded through the living room that Clay had stacked with books and stood in Scott's spot at the counter. "Where should I put them?"

I reached to take a box, but she wouldn't release it because I was pregnant, and nobody lets pregnant people do anything strenuous.

The car seat fit in the closet, but there wasn't any place to put the stroller except the middle of the living room. "It's fine for now," I told the sister. "We'll figure something out."

I grabbed a beer and pretended to chug. Then I handed it to her. She didn't react.

We sat outside on the lawn chairs and watched the kids play tag. They were chasing each other, but then they weren't. They were running without a pattern and their mouths opened, and the sound rose like a mist, but loud and rattling. Even watching, the Roar came from nowhere and everywhere. Jeremy's sister didn't scream along, but she closed her eyes when it started and put her head back. I started liking her more, which was horrible timing. I brought Goldie out there too. She didn't make any noise but flapped at her cage when they all started screaming. She settled down quickly after the train passed.

Eventually I noticed Jeremy's sister wasn't drinking her beer, and I wondered if I was supposed to know that she didn't drink.

She must have seen me eyeing the can. "Yeah, I'm not drinking, either." She laughed, but it came out like a snort, and then we both giggled at the snort. "I'm not sure yet, but I might be pregnant, too."

I just stared.

"Weird, huh? I haven't taken a test yet, so I could be wrong." She still held the beer can and fiddled with the opened tab. "Please don't tell anyone."

Jeremy was only 20 then, but his sister was much older. Maybe 35? I was 22.

"So the kids'll be cousins?"

"Yeah, maybe they'll be best friends, too." This was

sappier than I'd expected from her. It was a moment I was supposed to connect with her, but I didn't think I should. She left pretty soon after that.

Also, I've always hated coincidences, which is what I thought this was. They either mean everything or nothing.

I know this was the beginning of the 21st century already, but we didn't have internet in the trailer. Clay never bothered to set it up because he had it at work. You'd think I could at least steal some, but no luck there either.

Since this was before anybody had smartphones, I couldn't even look up the symptoms and side effects of my condition unless I trekked to the library or something, which I never felt like doing. I didn't want strangers reading over my shoulder, either. It didn't matter much—except my imaginary prego-symptoms might have been more accurate.

When I heard the Roar, I would imagine a tiny stirring inside me—like the baby howling along. It was frightening and uplifting at the same time.

Clay must have been going through some sort of spiritual crisis. Forty days in the desert or whatever. He'd sit silent and alone and drink beer after beer. He'd tuck an armload of them into the cracks of the recliner so he wouldn't have to go to the kitchen, and he'd drink them all even if they got warm. Then he'd stack the cans in tall towers around the edges of the recliner.

"Clay, is it a sin to get drunk?" I asked him once.

"Only if you're pregnant."

"Asshole."

When I talked to my mom on the phone, one of the ways to keep her from asking annoying questions was to ask her annoying questions.

"So how's Florida?" I'd been there plenty of times, but my idea of it didn't go past palm trees and pastel condos with seashells as decorations.

"The weather is beautiful. Thanks for asking."

"So what do you do there all day?"

"Oh, I don't know. Stuff."

"Stuff?"

"Yeah, stuff. I walk on the beach, and I get coffee in town. There's a cute little bookstore that I go to if it's raining, or else I go shopping."

"What does Dad do?" I asked.

"He reads the paper. He watches baseball on TV. Sometimes he comes on walks with me."

"He does?"

"Yes, quite a lot, actually."

"I can't picture that."

"We go out to eat, too."

"I can picture that."

And then usually Clay would start shouting at the radio or the TV, so I would hang up and pretend we got disconnected.

I should have worried about insurance with my impending baby, but I wasn't really thinking about that either. I was still on my parents' insurance, I thought. I didn't want to ask because it might get them suspicious.

The neighborhood was supposedly mobile. It was

a trailer park. All of the houses could roll down the highway. There should have been asphalt with a parking lot grid painted out and cars lined up parallel to each other. Except some of us would have got the zoom spot and be facing outward. The rest of us would have our butt-ends to the world.

Instead, we formed winding drives and circular little cul-de-sacs. In the center, there was a swing set—a nice wooden one with monkey bars, tire swing, and slide. There was an open area, perfect for kickball, behind the trailer park on the outside. So we were mobile in a committed, not-going-anywhere kind of way.

Ever since Clay was in the seminary, he always needed to live with lots of people. I don't claim to know how his mind works, but I notice things. When he quit the priest school, he started regular college and lived first in a dorm and then in a frat. After college, he rented a house with his brothers. People came and went—men, women, dogs even. He got screwed on the rent a lot. I don't know why he didn't move into the absolutely free trailer sooner. I had Jeremy before the breakup, but Clay just had a bunch of weirdoes. Maybe he was ministering to them or something.

I could tell he was lonely, but I wasn't sure what I was supposed to do about it.

By October, I'd stop in my tracks whenever I felt a train approach, whenever the windows shook and the empty beer cans clattered off the kitchen counter. I'd arch my back and lift my chin to the sky or the ceiling. I'd try to be subtle about it when I was with company, but my body would still respond.

Maybe the stars told Jeremy he wasn't a father. Or the crystals. Maybe he expected a shimmer in his aura that didn't come or a visit from his spirit animal. I liked the mystical side of Jeremy but never understood it. He didn't have a right to it—it was all appropriation and awful, but I didn't think about those things then.

"Why do you eat so much ice cream?" Scott asked me one day as he was snapping the buckles on his briefcase. Also, I'd left the freezer door open so I could eat the ice cream with my head wedged inside.

I pulled my head out of the freezer. "I like it," I said.

"You're going to get fat," he said.

"I know."

"You don't mind?"

"I'm about to get really fat anyway," I told him. "I'm *supposed* to get fat."

Scott lifted his eyebrows and gave his bowtie a slight tug.

"I'm pregnant," I told him, leaning forward and raising the volume of my voice. Then I remembered Scott was just a little kid, and my face started to get hot. I didn't know what to say next, so I stuck my head back in the freezer and licked my spoon.

Scott didn't react. He went home, and I thought about how I was a horrible person.

The next day, Scott carried his briefcase in the same as usual, all business. He took out a stack of papers, a textbook, and a mechanical pencil.

I was at the freezer again with an overloaded spoon of ice cream.

Scott snapped his briefcase shut and then snapped each of the buckles. He looked up, jerked into eye contact, and asked, "Are you married?"

"No."

"But you're having a baby?"

"Yes."

"Oh."

Scott was really good at these intense conversations about exactly one thing. You knew he was thinking about what you said.

"Is that okay?" Scott asked.

His conversational style was unnerving enough that I couldn't lie to him. I could sometimes steer the discussion elsewhere, but when he was in a particular mood, I couldn't even do that.

"Jesus, don't act all innocent. Look at the neighborhood, for God's sake!" I told him.

I hope no one expects this story to mean anything or come to some important conclusion. I'm just telling about the things that happened during the time that I thought I was pregnant but really wasn't.

Jeremy came by one day. He brought a mobile to hang over the crib. He'd made it himself. That kid breaks my heart.

"Jen. How *are* you?" His voice was all breathy, as usual, and there was this stick of hair that kept falling into his face, and he kept putting it back behind his ear. Plus he was holding this glittery contraption, stars falling down and tangling, his arm reaching far out from his body so none of the constellations would smoosh up against him.

I had a big wet snotball hovering behind my nose and mouth, then all hot behind my eyes, so I didn't say anything. I shook my head and hiccupped. I didn't want him back, but I didn't want him gone either, really.

After he left, I had a real moody fit for the next couple days. I cried all the time and only ate what I could spoon into my mouth directly from the box or carton or jug. Clay thought I was losing it. I didn't tell him I'd seen Jeremy. I told him it must be hormones.

"Jen, you need to see a doctor," Clay said.

"Yeah, yeah. I'll make an appointment." I had no intention of doing it.

I was living in a kind of limbo then. As long as nothing was confirmed, it wasn't quite real. I was playing house, and it was fun and miserable at the same time.

I don't really like it when Goldie sings. I think it's annoying, and she does it all the time. But I still take care of her. Ever since that time, every place I move, I carry her in her dirty little cage. Even now, years later.

I got in the habit of standing with my belly thrust forward and one hand on the small of my back. It seemed like the classic pregnant stance.

"I hate to say I'm disappointed in you." My mom said this to me on the phone.

I was on the lawn chair with iced tea, but the ice had melted, and it was gross. "Yeah, yeah. You're disappointed in me."

"Well, I'm not really."

"You just said it."

"I'm worried about you."

"Of course you are," I said. What was her job if it wasn't to worry about me?

"You haven't even looked for a job."

"I looked a little bit."

"Jen, why haven't you looked harder?"

"Well, for one thing, it's October. They don't need new teachers in October."

"You never know."

"Yes, Mom, I do know. The Caterville school district hires in August. So does Clifton. So does Geneva—." I ducked inside because the Roar was starting, but it didn't much help. I missed the next thing she said.

"—or someone might quit."

"Bernsburg, Fort Wayne," I said. "All of the schools around here. Even the private schools."

"Someone could get fired."

"I don't think so."

"Or get sick or have a baby."

"Why don't you ever worry about Clay like this?"

"What's wrong with Clay?"

"I don't know. Nothing." He was passed out on the recliner in the mobile home where he squatted, for one thing.

"You could be a substitute."

"Mom, subbing is the worst job on Earth."

"Then you'd already know people for next year. And they'd know you, too, Jen, and they'd hire you right away," my mom said.

"I didn't go to college to be a babysitter."

Sometime in November I began joining the Roar—just a low hum—under my breath.

Scott was over every day by then. I'd force myself to be cheerful for the time it took him to do his homework. He worked standing at the kitchen counter. He'd leave his bowtie on but unfasten his shirt's top button, so it sort of bunched his collar into a ruff. I would try to make sure the counter wasn't sticky before he started.

It was hard not to believe Jeremy when he said he wasn't a father. I hadn't had sex with anyone else, but it did seem like something he would know. He wasn't the type to lie.

My not wanting to talk about myself got my mom talking about herself more than I ever remember her doing. It was uncomfortable.

"You know, coming down here has been really great for your dad and me."

"That's great."

"We don't fight anymore."

"Yeah, right."

"No, really. We get along great."

"Well that's great." I didn't believe her, but whatever. "I'm glad to hear it."

"It's the atmosphere. It's very romantic."

"Romantic?" That was not the word I expected.

"Yes, it's very romantic. Brings back the spark, you know. The old feelings."

"Mom, I don't think...."

"Your dad and I are spending a lot of time together again. When it rains in the afternoon, you know."

"Mom, I'd rather not hear this." It was just like them to get along now, when it didn't even matter.

"No, I guess not." She sighed. "I just forget sometimes—it's so nice talking to you lately. But of course there are things you don't want to hear."

"Yeah, I don't. I'm sorry."

Mostly Clay ignored me, but every once in a while he'd take an interest.

"When are you going to tell Mom about your predicament?" he asked. He used his priest voice and raised his eyebrows up and down and up again.

"I'm not quite ready to re-explain the Immaculate Conception, you know?" I was trying to be funny, I guess. It's not like my parents thought I was all pure or anything.

"God, it's so annoying when people fuck that up. Everybody does it." Clay was still talking like Father Holiness even though he was swearing.

"What?"

"The Immaculate Conception did involve sex. It was the conception of Mary—not Jesus. You're such a dumbass."

"What are you talking about?"

"No original sin. Mary was conceived and born without original sin, and that's why it was immaculate."

"You know what I mean. You don't have to go preacher on me."

"You know, you've got an extra little piece of sin inside you now."

I could feel the extra piece of sin, but only if I bent my knees slightly, furrowed my eyebrows, and really concentrated. It was stronger when the kids howled.

Clay would have made a horrible priest. You can't go around telling pregnant people they have extra bits of sin inside them—even the unwed ones. Even the ones who aren't really pregnant.

I liked Scott mostly because he was kind of pathetic in the way he acted grownup and pretentious. He could never quite time the playground Roar. He wouldn't start until the others were nearly wound down and the train was almost past, and then his shriek let loose. He would stop as soon as he heard himself and turn bright red. He'd stick his hands in his pockets then or tug at his elastic bowtie and mumble about how strange all those kids were.

Jeremy used to meditate all the time when I lived with him. He'd turn off the TV or radio, then sit on the floor, wedged between the couch and a card table we used for eating. It was important that I was quiet, too, and didn't touch him at all. At first, I had a deep respect for it and would even try to join him in trance world, from the couch with my legs pulled up. But one day I noticed he had a boner, while supposedly gone from the physical world. Maybe that's normal, but it made me suspicious.

Goldie eventually died, so it's actually a different bird I lug around now.

Clay never seemed startled by the Roar. He'd keep up whatever he was doing—folding socks, or watching football, or reading the Bible. Sometimes his smile would twist deeper into his cheeks, but that was it.

I couldn't get him to admit it was anything weird or even a recurring phenomenon.

"Yeah, sometimes the kids scream," he'd tell me with his "infinite patience" voice from priest camp.

"All together," I'd insist. "When the train comes."

"Yeah, sometimes the train is loud like that, too."

He infuriated me then. Well, really, he infuriated me always. Growing up, he would claim an equal number of pizza slices even if he wasn't hungry enough to eat them. And if his shoe came untied, we'd have to stop right there, even if the bus was coming, while he fixed it.

I hummed along, quietly, to every Roar until December or so, when, if I happened to be alone in the trailer, I'd let myself get a little louder. As the cabinet doors crashed open and closed and the loose tiles rattled in the bathroom, it was like the train's rumbling also made a vacuum hose that sucked at the air in my lungs. But it was the kid's voices, too, and maybe it was feeling like I was meant to join them. Still, I held back. I experimented with different pitches, and I'd open my mouth, but I'd only howl at a conversational volume.

"Hey, Scott?" Scott was already seated on the bottom end of the teeter-totter. Both hands on the handlebar.

"How come you never want to come out here before it gets dark?" The sky was still burning orange over the trees far off, but most of the trailers' "porch" lights were on, and we were the only ones on the playground.

Scott shrugged, and I climbed on about halfway to the fulcrum. The teeter-totter didn't move, so I inched backward.

"We should come out earlier," I said. "It gets cold with the sun down."

"That's good," Scott called out, and he pushed off pretty hard. I reached behind me for the handle just in time.

"Do you know about infinity?" he asked, loudly.

"What about it?"

"You know that it goes on forever?"

"If you come out during the day, you could play with other kids, and I could sit on the bench."

"Infinity plus one is still infinity."

"Yep." I didn't know what infinity had to do with anything, but I thought Scott might be avoiding other kids, and I was mean enough to try to find out why. "Do you know the kids who play out here?"

"Of course I do." He rolled his eyes. "And infinity minus one is infinity too. That's even weirder."

"If you did this with another *kid* it would balance better."

"I thought I have to do my homework."

"You could do it after." I was up.

"Whatever." Scott pushed off, and I was down again.

"Fine. Whatever." I was a little ill from the motion of it all, the ups and downs of the teeter-totter and the bumps on either end.

Then I was up again, and Scott hopped off, and I dropped—hard—to the ground. "You little bastard!" I clutched my gut and rolled off the teeter-totter. I couldn't feel anything too weird there, but I wasn't sure what I was feeling for.

Scott came to where I was kneeling on the ground. He put his hand on my shoulder. "Jen, I am so sorry. I didn't mean to do that. I mean, I did mean to, but I forgot about the baby... and I didn't think you'd hit so hard."

I stood up slowly. I felt a little stunned, slightly nauseous, but otherwise okay. Scott wasn't crying, but was probably about to.

"I'm okay. But we have to go inside now."

I started toward my trailer, and Scott galloped beside me.

"I'm really sorry." He was out of breath. "Are you sure you're okay?" I was half-ignoring him, but he didn't stop talking. "You called me a bastard."

"Sorry." I was probing my abdomen, trying to decide whether or not it hurt. "Don't tell anyone I said that, okay?"

"Okay. But will you tell me what it means?"

He caught my attention then. "Do you know what the other bad words mean?" I asked.

"Only shit. Will you tell me the rest of them, too?"

I could see why Scott was embarrassed to hang out

with the kids on the playground.

"I'll tell you what everything means. Let's go inside."

"Wait a minute. What about infinity minus infinity?" Scott trotted along beside me. "Would that be infinity, too?"

Another thing about Jeremy's meditations. I watched, so I know with one hundred percent certainty that he never moved a muscle. But somehow his hair would get messed up as he sat there.

I started eating the weird food that pregnant people are supposed to crave. Pickles with chocolate and other combinations. Maybe that was what caused my morning sickness.

Goldie was originally Jeremy's canary, but he gave him to me when I moved out. Just packed him into my car with my clothes and my CDs. He said it felt right, and I didn't argue because I sort of got along with Goldie. Besides, Jeremy was so fucking nice about the whole thing. And I couldn't leave the bird with someone so nice.

"So, Clay, when you left the seminary, why did you?"

"Why'd I what?" Clay was propped on his recliner as usual, listening to the radio. When he listened to the radio, he tended to look at it instead of at me even if I was talking to him.

"Why'd you leave?" I got into the habit of looking at the radio when I talked to him, too.

"I just didn't want to do it anymore."

"Did you have a crisis of faith?"

"No."

"Did you question the Church?"

"Not really." He was still looking at the radio. It made more sense when it was the TV.

"Did you freak out about not ever getting married or doing normal stuff?"

"Nah."

"Was it sex?"

"No, Jen, it wasn't sex."

"Well? Did you get kicked out or something?"

"I wasn't sure. I don't know. I might even go back someday." He turned to look at me for a second or two this time but didn't stay focused.

I was focused on him now, however. "Wow. Are you thinking about going back?"

"Kind of. But probably not for a while."

"Can you still?" I asked.

"Can I go back?"

"Yeah, can you still go back?"

"Of course I can. I said I wasn't kicked out."

I used to try to meditate with Jeremy, but every time something would start to itch, and I'd have to scratch it. Also I've never been good at keeping my eyes closed.

Being pregnant was a great excuse to cry all the time. It was an even better excuse than the fact that my boyfriend thought I cheated on him and didn't even mind so I had to leave him and move in with my weird holy brother who was hiding out in the mobile home our parents bought and then abandoned. All of that was sad, but funny, too, and it made me too exhausted to cry when

I thought about it.

When the train came, I really wanted to howl like the kids—the baby wanted to Roar, I told myself. The threaded voices were like arms or like that vacuum hose that sucked at something in my throat or deeper. It rattled in my chest and in my gut and even my hair stood on end. But I fought hard not to let myself. I fought hard not to fall over.

"You aren't getting any fatter," Scott told me one day utterly out of the blue.

"Well, thanks," I said.

"I mean your face is, but not your belly."

"Great."

"Aren't you supposed to be having a baby?" He looked right at me as he talked, like he almost always did.

"Yeah." I was kind of watching kids play out the window. They put me on edge.

"Aren't you supposed to be getting fat?"

"I guess. Maybe not yet."

"Maybe? You guess? Aren't you supposed to know?"

"Hmm?"

"You never know any of the stuff you're supposed to know. You're a grown-up, but you don't know anything. You know what bad words mean and that's it. You hardly even know more math than me."

"That's bullshit."

"I told my mom you called me a bastard. She said you'd know all about it, she guessed, but she wasn't really mad."

"Scott! Why'd you tell her?"

"She was going on to Mrs. Nelson about how great you are to me."

"Well, that's a lie." I meant about Scott's mom saying I was great. I didn't think any of his story was true after he said that.

"She can't believe you watch me for so cheap."

"Ugh."

"Why do you watch me for less than minimum wage?"

"I don't."

"Do you even know what minimum wage is?"

He had me there.

"Do you have ulterior motives?"

"Sure, I'm gonna kill you and sell your body parts to science. I'll be rich."

"Nope. You'd miss me too much if I was dead or didn't come over."

"No, I wouldn't."

For Christmas, Clay and I agreed on the lie I should tell our parents the next time I talked to Mom.

"You know, your dad and I are coming home on the twenty-second this year."

"Yes, Mom, I know."

"Could you stop by the trailer and turn the heat on in the morning? I get so cold now that I'm used to Florida."

"Got it."

"Good." She paused. "Will Jeremy come with us for the holiday or with his family?"

"He's going to be with his family."

"But you'll come."

"Yeah, actually, I think I'm going to stay with you in the trailer."

"With us? That will be great."

"Clay, too," I said.

"And Clay?"

"Yeah, I saw him the other day, and we talked about spending the whole week there—like old times, you know?" Of course, we'd never all stayed in the trailer. We'd had a house then even if it was small and kind of crappy. I didn't miss losing crayons down the heating ducts or the smell of them when they melted or the tug of war on the bathroom door handle, but I did miss that it was settled, that our family just was. The house was stuck to the ground, and we were stuck in it, and that was that.

"It will be crowded."

"We'll be fine. Just like old times."

This is going to sound pathetic, but there was this actor on a soap opera that I used to have dreams about—just dreams—when I was living with Jeremy. I didn't really pay attention to his character, but he had a long ponytail and was very sexy.

On my rational days, I knew the imaginary fetus was Jeremy's, but on others, it seemed like one of these steamy dreams had taken hold. Sometimes I'd sit on the couch in the afternoons and watch this guy. I wondered if my baby would have a ponytail like his.

I couldn't picture the kid beyond the ponytail. If I tried, a different kid popped into my brain, a different kid every time, one from the Roar, face warped and howling.

Christmas shopping was awful that year, and I was panicky the whole time. I drove to the mall every third day when my car started. I'd walk into stores and wait for inspiration to hit me, but nothing ever did. If a salesperson approached, I walked the other way. I had that about-to-cry feeling whenever I was in a store but never actually cried.

On the last day I bought a random bunch of trinkets. I didn't know what would go to who. I figured I'd wrap them, and then maybe forgetting what was inside would make the decision easier.

I wondered if my Baptism was negated because this little piece of original sin had crept back inside me.

"Will the baby drag me to Limbo if I die?" I asked Clay.

He rolled his eyes. "Where do you come up with this shit, Jen? Nobody talks about Limbo anymore."

But I thought it sounded better than Hell.

Clay drove to the airport to pick up our parents while I stayed home to get the place ready. I hadn't gotten around to cleaning the bathroom or the kitchen the night before. I hadn't wrapped the presents yet or put up the tree. Everything was a mess.

First I put the gifts in boxes, then I sprayed down the shower, then I washed the dishes in the sink. I let the words "I'm pregnant I'm pregnant I'm pregnant" run through my mind. I was practicing for when my mom got home.

I was in the kitchen, wiping down the countertop, when I heard a train coming, far off. Plates rattled in the open cabinets. Goldie flapped, and I grabbed the edge of the sink. The words in my head blended with the voices outside, and I let the Roar swallow me. I threw back my head, and I wailed.

That Roar lasted a long time. It was the train's noise and the screams from outside and my own voice and also the thoughts inside my brain. Each one was louder than all the others somehow, and my skin itched, and my stomach twisted. My bones rattled, I think, and also that Roar lasted so long it might still be going. When I stopped screaming, my throat was raw, and my whole body was exhausted.

When my family arrived, I was still in my sweatpants. I'm sure they could tell I'd been crying.

Clay always had incense burning in that place. It wasn't like the little sticks and cones that Jeremy burned. It was heavier and smokier and holier. So the trailer always smelled like church. Clay insisted it smelled like bird.

As soon as my mom entered that dirty cramped space, I told her. I pushed her to the chair, and I dropped to the floor and put my head on her knees. I told her I was pregnant.

Then, I don't know, I might have cried some more, but I felt better.

Goldie's not really gold, you know. She's more camel-colored. Or brighter than that, I guess, but not the color I expect a canary to be.

It was the biggest relief in the world, when I climbed onto the examination table, to let my mom speak for me.

"She thinks she's pregnant, but she hasn't had a test. She hasn't had a period since the first week of August."

I just laid back and let them figure it out for me.

And of course, it turned out that I wasn't pregnant.

Maybe I lost the baby when I joined the Roar. Sometimes, I think it could have escaped then. It could have flown out when I let everything else go. Or else I never had it.

That was all so long ago. I still don't know what it means. Goldie, who was a finch after all, Jeremy and his sister, Clay on his recliner, Scott crashing the teeter-totter, my mom's voice on the phone...they were all real. But now that they're gone, just like that imaginary baby, could they have been? I only have one piece of that time. It's the Roar that still wells up in me furiously, out of nowhere, with no warning, and it doesn't mean shit.

Nutsacks in Space

Here in space, my nutsack doesn't sag. Just, there it is, full and round, or sometimes thin, almost translucent, the testicles inside it bulbs of matter pulsing through wrinkled skin. If I bat at my nutsack, gently of course, the dent will stay where I've poked it. I am not alone in playing with my nutsack, though I am alone in my bubble, my soft and transparent orb of plastic. We must be naked in our bubbles because all our skin is required for communication. No sound passes from bubble to bubble, even in collision, even in the ricochet to nowhere. There is not much to do out here, bouncing around in an air-packed bubble. No one to talk to. No books to read. No baseball to follow. I see the nutsacks of everyone else, of all who have nuts in my section of un-sectioned space. Each one twisting in their bubble to inspect each nut twisting in its sack. We are free about looking, which is good because the eye is drawn there naturally, just as it is to the free-floating breasts of some others. My bubble's hatch is triangular, not compatible with the lower class bubbles. Though my bubble is not a luxury model. Some are lost every day, bounced off the fringes, but we can't count how many. I can't stretch my arms full over my head while my legs are straight—only if I crunch my knees. No sound passes through the vacuum. In the bubble, it would be unbearable to release a sound that would bounce forever. I can stand, but what is standing? It is lying. It is hanging upside down. Those with small bubbles always scrunch, fetal like a baby, cradled by their plastic and by all of space. Hours ago, or days, or weeks, there was one: a large clear bubble. A person inside, a glorious form. *We will collide. Can we connect? Can we share our air or press a finger through to touch? Touch! Another membrane. Bouncing inside the clear casing of autonomous bubble. Her skin is red and translucent. The blood rushes in her. An entire body, held up to the light. We will intersect. She rolls. She spins. Frantic in her space. Her space! Her hatch is square. It's large enough for jumping jacks. She kicks. Inverts. Her skin screams panic! I'd share air and fingertip. I would. I would.* We bumped. My plastic concaved to her vex. But our hatches didn't match, triangle to square. Triangle to square. I bounced outward. There are lines on my nutsack. I know them well. It is my only toy. Twists through the skin, they haven't faded yet. Torsion trails and wrinkle indentations. Left from Earth-living, when gravity pulled. How long has it been since I've hooked hatches? How long since I've seen another bubble? Even a small one? An inner being, cramped and fetal? But I don't think I'm at the edge. I don't think I've been lost.

From the Multiverse Chronicles

The nature of friendship changed world to world. We were like sisters in this one, not lovers or best friends or arbitrarily paired research associates. Maybe we were like two puppies in a puppy pile. But of course we also talked about science and discovery and if this life were the one, the keeper.

You have to understand. It was all yogurt in this world, plain yogurt, and nothing else, nothing at all.

I liked the softness. I liked that I didn't question, or only briefly, how the yogurt didn't spoil. Not past the spoilage that is already yogurt, I mean. Where it came from was never a question. It only increased. It was never a question of any world, though folks may query through the comms.

Sleeping was an immediate obstacle. A body submerged was cool and soft, but the head must stay above for breathing. We took turns, one holding the other's head aloft for a full eight hours. It was tender, but it couldn't be sustained. Then we discovered a pattern to form with our bodies, of my head atop Marta's thigh, and her body curled like the moon too, and her head on my thigh. Clockwise for the first four hours, then a flip and a turn, and counter for the remaining four.

Circadian rhythms held, though the light never changed, and time was pale and soft, too.

For hygiene we arranged our quarters in three parts, drawn only in the mind. We slept in an area distinct from where we ate, which was also distinct from where we defecated. We hoped so. But alas, as our bodies took in nothing but yogurt, our releases merged in color and texture with the world around us. There was no shape or stain to orient ourselves upon waking, no landmark in the mush. Oh, for a compass!

Submerged in the yogurt we reminisced, in the beginning, of other worlds, other explorations. A world of dragons—we took notes. An ocean world—we built a raft. A bureaucratic world—we shared lunch and gossip, rolled our eyes. A broken-glass world—the only softness was Marta's body until that turned sharp and jagged, too.

But there was peace in the yogurt, in waking to a world of pale nothing, to softness, to calm. It stilled our stories. Against the nothing was just our bodies, and there was the way her body came to seem like my body, too.

Were there ever others on this world? Beings in the yogurt, or from it? I felt we could live forever. As we consumed nothing but yogurt, we'd turn into it slowly, just as our shit had. We'd merge into each other and into this world and just be and just be satisfied.

The yogurt was soft, and we were quiet, and we were calm.

Then, in the blankness, a thought emerged. Not in me, but in Marta.

She wondered how we didn't sink.

I haven't mentioned the sky or what was the horizon. It was colorless. The line between yogurt and atmosphere was far off and hazy. Only seen, or not even seen, but sensed. A shift in consistency. Gravity still pulled. That was certain in the sag of our breasts, the weight of our feet. The feel of up was accompanied by heat. And the feel of down was met with chill.

I imagined something like cold steel deep below the yogurt.

Marta was not sure. Then neither was I.

And so we dug. And yet digging through yogurt! It was impossible. It was absurd. We had no shovel, but our hands worked as scoops. But how to keep the slop from sliding? No sooner was it dug away than it oozed back to fill the hole. There was no bucket. There was no way to form a pile. It was perfect yogurt flatness, flatness that fought to keep itself.

Marta dug and slid in the hole, and the yogurt slid around her. The hole didn't keep, but some days she kept herself inside it, pointing toes as far as they could go and begging me to press from the top, to push her head down, to make her body a stake, push her toes to reach further.

"Please," she said. "We have to know."

So I did. I pushed on her shoulders, then her head. Then we twisted and squirmed our way deeper. I pushed until she couldn't hold her breath, and I was submerged too. We couldn't breathe. I pulled her up.

She gasped and heaved. I sputtered, spewed yogurt.

I could only see her for the eyes that were dark against the yogurt as she opened them and wiped, with a yogurt hand, against them, and smeared yogurt against yogurt, until the darkness of her mouth split from the yogurt lump that was her head.

I'm sure I looked the same.

Marta gave up her digging. But still in her sleep she burrowed, and we'd wake in airlessness. It was panic to wake submerged in yogurt—which direction to scramble? We'd jolt, and there was silent screaming until we found air. Bright lovely gulps of air. Before nesting again, half submerged.

The yogurt didn't sting our eyes anymore, but we couldn't see through it. Years passed. Those must have been years.

And anyway, what use to see through it? There was only more yogurt. Our bodies were covered with it, and it was only rare moments, struck by nostalgia or something else, that we scraped to check the color of our skin, not knowing whose we'd find beneath the yogurt, or how pale and milk-like it would be.

We never let go of each other. As we rolled through the yogurt, a clasp of fingers would circle a wrist or an ankle. Whose? Or elbows would tangle. Or knees.

We'd sleep, and we'd eat, and we'd release yogurt from our bodies. And we'd talk, sometimes with words, but mostly now without them.

And the yogurt increasing.

One time we woke, the fingers circled the wrist that wasn't—the wrong one! Marta wasn't me. I knew it, and I knew the fingers I held were my fingers, and where was Marta? Asleep beside me.

And then I knew we'd have to leave.

FastDog Security

Bus Station

The inside of the station is brightly lit. It makes the outside, through the window, darker. The 9:40 bus to Grand Rapids will pull through any minute and bounce shadows on the wall behind me. The bus will zip over the highway like a bug to a zapper to this station that floats on empty winter fields.

Before that happens, a woman walks into the station. She's young, with all sorts of extra makeup around her eyes. She stops short at my checkpoint, her face inches from mine.

"Oh!" She hops backward.

"Do you have a ticket?" I say.

"Yes, sir." She pulls something from her purse, and a speck of gray fluff falls to the floor.

"Oh, I don't need to see it." The wooden stick is smooth in my hand. The metal-detecting wand is quiet on the table. "I need to check your bags and your person. Could you please open those up?" She does, and I rifle through six—six!—bags.

Clutter

through sweaters, books, tangled cords, lacy underthings, through tubes and plastic cases, bottles and combs, brushes, colored pencils, crumpled Kleenex

Bus Station

"Now, Miss," I say. Her raccoon-ring eyes look back at me. "It's not my business, but I just can't see someone pretty like you needing all these beauty supplies. There's room now that we're only in Botkins, but once you reach LaGrange and then Kalamazoo, the bus will fill up, and you'll be crushed. Wouldn't it be better to have less stuff?"

She rolls those smudgy eyes and takes a step.

"Miss?" I place my body between her and the gate. "Please put your bags down and hold out your arms. I'm going to wave this little wand in front of you. Car keys out of your pockets?"

The wand beeps at the heels of her boots, which she bends to unlace. She grunts but doesn't speak. I poke at the boots, then she shoves her feet back in.

The bus will be here any minute, but she collapses onto the bench, past the security border, the banquet tables I've flipped to make a barrier, and she spreads her bags around her. Her purse stays on her lap, but its contents dump to the floor.

Clutter

wadded tissues, chapstick, phone and charger, pencil stubs, ticket stubs, receipts, candy wrappers, loose and chipped M&Ms, hair brush, fluff, lint, a crushed mini package of cheese-and-peanut-butter crackers

So much trash—it's bleeding into the checker pattern of the floor tiles.

It's my wife, Rosie, at home with her purse spilling open. It's all the stuff nobody needs that overwhelms us.

Bus Station

Finally, through the window, there are flashes, far off, sparking toward us along the flat of the highway. Headlights brush over the slush in the parking lot, then shoot into empty fields and sit still. Before I can help, the woman has gathered her six bags, hugging them to her body like a second, bunchy coat. My breath catches, but nothing drops. Only the paper scraps already on the floor, her dust and debris, whoosh as she shuffles over them.

As the bus rumbles away, dragging its lights into and then out of the windows, I finish the last of my work. I lock the wand and wooden stick in the supply closet, flip the tables to stand upright. I sweep the last trail of crumbs and metallic flakes of candy wrapper. The old station is empty, echoing, comforting—there's room to breathe again.

It's not a paid position I hold. Just volunteer security.

Rosie

I drive home, watching for a low constellation that glows at the horizon. It's a cluster of five houses, huddled together on the empty fields. Porch lights. Front windows. A mile past where the gas station and the fire station sit catty corner to each other.

My house is the last one, and Rosie is inside. She's left the kitchen light on, and there's also a low glow from the bedroom window. She'll be glowing, too, and the bed will be warm and tucked neatly around the edges.

But I have to check her car first and see to the clutter she's grown. Under the seat is a crumpled coffee cup, a receipt for gas. In the ashtray is a single cigarette butt because she still smokes just the one on the way home from work, and every evening I remove it for her. Driving gloves on the passenger seat are crumpled until I fold them. A stray pillowcase has fallen into the backseat. I bring it inside.

Bus Station

It's the next day, and my boots echo when I click over the tile of the station floor. When I tap my wooden stick on the table leg, the sound booms.

The only other person who works here is Gressley, spiky hair and plastic glasses. He's at his ticket window, clacking away at his computer. There's no telling if it's porn or video games he's at or if it's whatever he gets paid to do. There are four people past the barrier, luggage stacked around them—I already searched it—waiting for the 2:56 to Muncie.

My four tables are flipped on their sides, like always. Their smooth, long surfaces face the entrance, and the legs point to the boarding area. One card table is upright, but no bags are dumped now. All that clutter is scooped into purses and duffels and backpacks. The ones clutched by the passengers who are waiting.

And then there's one more ticket holder at my checkpoint.

"You could fit all this stuff into one bag," I tell the woman. My wooden stick is tangling in the shredded tissues at the bottom of her purse, then fluffing with lint in an empty suitcase.

"Oh, but I'm going *shopping*," she says. "I'll use the space for the things I buy."

Things. They all want things.

I scrabble through them.

It's only eight months this station has even had a security guard, volunteer or otherwise. I'm the first at Botkins, Indiana FastDog Terminal. Before I got here, anybody could board the bus. So long as Gressley sold them a ticket, that is.

The Wand

I zap my wand at the aluminum legs of my flipped tables sometimes just to see the light and hear the beep. Or I point it at my own boots with their steel toes. It keeps me busy between the buses.

Clutter

In the eighteen months after I retired from the plant but before I started at FastDog—that's when I had time to get organized.

First, the pantry in the kitchen. It wasn't my business, since Rosie does the shopping and the cooking. But that doesn't mean the clutter never got to me. Labels facing all directions and duplicates of everything. So I cleaned it out. Donated the second and third cans of lima beans, tomato paste, artichokes, pears in heavy syrup. Wiped down the shelves and put some order to the just-one-of-each rest of it.

And Rosie's clothes. She had them sorted by color, but that didn't make sense. I pulled all the sweaters together and all the t-shirts. Then I purged her of duplicates. Except for socks. Of course, I left two of each color of socks.

Since I started at FastDog, there's been less time for keeping back the clutter. But I don't complain. Rosie's nephew is a big shot muckety-muck for the company. He got me the volunteer position, and it's an important one.

Clutter

playing cards, crossword puzzles, pharmaceuticals, laptop computers, water bottles, padlocks, airplane pillows, chewed gum, fresh gum, gum stuck in wads of pocket lint, whole packs of gum, loose Chiclets, checkbooks, textbooks, hairy wads of gunk stuck to the bottoms of purses and the insides of pockets

Rosie

Rosie makes beds all day, replaces towels, and bosses the other housekeepers at the Holiday Haven who are making beds and replacing towels.

Head of housekeeping. She's seen some horrors.

Clutter

bloody sheets, broken bottles of mini-bar drinks, cracker crumbs like dandruff through the linens

Bus Station

Between buses, when no one is at my checkpoint or buying tickets at his window, I talk to Gressley. "Catch the end of the game last night?" I call out.

"I don't watch basketball."

I tell him about the game anyway, and he nods as he types. Then I ask if he wants to know what Rosie found in a hotel room yesterday. He perks up from his typing, and I wish it was weirder than a cell phone charger. It's what we talk about most, the stuff she finds. It's fun when neither of us can figure out what a thing is for. His guess is usually sex. I like to think of other possibilities.

A kid like Gressley should get out of this station instead of typing on his computer all day. It's only about a dozen people ever come through, and half already have their ticket from the first leg, when they bought round trip. Or maybe less than half, if folks bought on the internet. But I'm not sure Gressley is even working when he types, that spiky head bobbing. It might be video games.

Clutter

Rosie has found shark teeth, mega-phones, a bathtub full of unpopped popcorn, parking meter, half-melted snowmen, strings of sticky hot caramel wrapping out of the bathroom and down the hallway, clinging to the walls and floor and toilet seat.

Gressley gets bored hearing about the ordinary things, though.

toenail clippings, orange-tipped cotton swabs, tissues, cellophane ghosts, lipsticked plastic cups, socks, snaked out condoms, hangers, cell phone chargers

I'm checking for weapons mostly with the electric wand and the wooden stick. And other dangerous things like firecrackers and flammable liquids. They can take liquor and cigarettes, but I warn them not to drink or smoke while riding.

Open Space

Between the 2:56 to Muncie and the 6:04 to Dayton, there's time for a quick drive to the subdivision going in on the west side of Orrindale, past Huntoon, where Rosie and I live. The Freiburgers used to farm that land when the old man was alive.

Now there are lots laid out and a few finished houses blighting the ground that was once flat and open, only wind sweeping over soybeans or corn. Last week's snow has blown away except in cruddy spots against the lee-wall of each house. No one's building now, not in the cold.

The space between towns is shrinking. We're losing

the buffer. I like to keep an eye on the houses springing up, give them a hurtful stare.

Neither Huntoon or Orrindale or even Berlinda is as big as Botkins, which is big enough to have the FastDog bus terminal with a clerk but not big enough to have an airport like Clifton does, even though it is a tiny airport.

I check up to a dozen passengers a day, almost always strangers. It's too many and too crowded. There were never strangers at the plant, just the old crew.

I like small towns, but I like the spaces between them better.

Clutter

wingtips stuffed with wooden feet, tennis shoes with balled up sweat socks, cracked flip-flops, crumpled loafers, dirty work boots wrapped in plastic grocery bags

I didn't plan the retirement, but the time came, and it felt right. Better me than some young guy with a family. It's not that money is tight, but how long does it have to last? You never know.

A fellow could use a cane for a weapon. Also, he could use a cane to walk and be pretty out-of-sorts without one. So I give a cane the once over and let the carrier know not to strike anyone. I say it firm but friendly at the same time.

The Wand

The wand they gave me is electric. It beeps when it gets close to metal, and it buzzes and lights up. It's an older model but works fine.

Rosie

In the morning, Rosie comes into the bedroom out of the shower, wrapped in a bright white hotel towel, but her hair and legs are still dripping. Her skin is pink from the heat of the shower, and her cheeks glow like she is still young. She takes hold of me at the waist.

"Don't get me wet," I say.

Rosie giggles and flops onto the bed.

"Now the bed will be soggy."

"I'm changing it today anyway. The sheets, I mean."

"Oh." I bounce on the bed beside her, but far enough to stay dry.

She rolls over. Rosie's body is round in the middle. Full and smooth. She looks juicy with the shower still misty all over her. Her arms and legs, though, are thin and hard-muscled.

"What's got into you?"

"It was just a good shower. I'm in a good mood." She reaches out to pinch me. "You?"

I ease an arm into her towel. She smells delicious, but I'm not sure what either of us wants. "Do you have time?" I could be convinced.

She squeezes my hand. "Oh, not really." Rosie kisses my forehead and splatters me with water from her hair.

She dresses, then, and I watch, disappointed or maybe relieved. She puts herself back to middle aged, respectable. Her hair is dried and pinned. Her skin is toweled and lotioned and covered in polyester uniform slacks and button-down shirt. She powders the glow out of her face, then colors a different pink to it.

What if I grabbed her?

Now that she's done up, she'd be annoyed.

"Why are you watching me like that?"

"I don't know," I say.

We drink coffee then from the two mugs I saved, both different pretty colors.

Rosie and I don't have kids. We waited, and then it was too late. Rosie minds some, but I don't. There's too many people in the world already.

Bus Station

And then one day my wand isn't working. The hand-held metal detector. It occurs mid-shift, between the 2:56 and the 6:14 daily departures. It won't beep. It won't light up.

I un-hitch the back and take the batteries out for a shake. They aren't ordinary batteries like for a remote control or a flashlight. They look expensive. The supply closet has lots of toilet paper but no backup batteries.

I've been spending some of my downtime scanning the walls for bomb implants. In retrospect, now, that was not a bright idea.

I leave a voice message for Rosie's nephew, Phil: "This is your Uncle Hank. Volunteer security at Botkins bus depot. Listen, Phil, I've got a problem with my wand. The hand-held metal detector. I think it needs batteries, but I can't find a spare set. T9Y7674B is the model number and it wants 87A5WX batteries. That's T-9-Y-7-6-7-4-B on the wand and 8-7-A-5-W-X on the batteries."

There's two hours before the next departure, and I don't know what Phil will be able to do.

"Gressley. I'm going to run to the store." I walk to his window and wait for him to look up. "I need batteries."

He reaches for the 87A5WX battery that I've got in my hand. "You won't find this at the hardware store."

"Maybe the Super Walmart?"

He turns it over. "Hank, these are specialty batteries. They might not even make them anymore."

Gressley probably doesn't know what he's talking about, but the Super Walmart is a better bet than Umber's Hardware, so I drive twenty miles to Orrindale, just inside where Freiburger's farm/subdivision is.

Clutter

The Super Walmart has nine brands each of 4.5-volt, D, C, AA, AAA, AAAA, A23, 9-Volt, CR2032 and LR44. Most of the hooks have at least five packages hanging, with no less than two batteries per pack. There are batteries that look like a damn nickel and batteries that look like cans of gasoline. But no 87A5WX.

Open Space

I can't help swinging wide in my drive back to the station. Take the old roads through the countryside, only ten minutes out of my way, past Freiburger's old place again. I'm antsy, but I know there's time.

Bill Freiburger was in my class at school, and I used to eat supper sometimes with his family. I remember watching his dad eat. He was so tired you could feel it in the stillness around him. Still, it was fascinating, the amount of mashed potatoes he could swallow. He shut down every muscle but in the one arm for lifting his fork and his jaw for chewing. Even his eyelids would droop.

Bill was afraid of his dad, but I saw pride radiating from him. It seemed to be about the sweat he had put into his day. That's how all the old farmers were. And it was the same with my dad, home from the plant. Of course I couldn't see it then because I was so afraid of him. But I knew it for myself later.

Rosie

Sometimes, Rosie and I talk about the bags I check. I tell her how women cringe and turn red, how I can't help noticing personal items, then feel funny for looking at them.

"You don't even know what the embarrassing ones are!" She sinks into couch cushions, too many cushions for one tiny couch.

"Well, sometimes their bags are stinky."

"That might be embarrassing." The cushions are all over her. But they seem more like luxury than clutter. It's only because of Rosie. She is claiming them as herself as she nestles. "Like dirty underwear?"

"More like egg salad or bologna." I poke a finger into the softness of Rosie's middle. "People have food in their bags." I stroke her shoulder. "Not sex."

"They don't have sex in their bags?" She flips up her toes and sends the pillows into avalanche. Rosie slips away, into the couch, the pile of pillows. I want to squeeze her, but there are too many pillows between us.

Clutter

chocolate bars, potato chips, beef jerky, peanut butter and jelly sandwiches, Chinese takeout, chewy fruit candy, hard sugar candy, bananas, hard boiled eggs, crumbs, those little cups of pudding—punctured and oozing out through the underwear, paperback romance novels, and beauty products

Bus Station

Back at the station, Gressley is watching for me. "Phil called. He says to hold tight on the battery."

"Hold tight?"

"That's what he said."

"Super Walmart didn't have them. Neither did Umber's."

"I looked them up while you were out. You have to special order."

"Did Phil say—"

"—He just said 'hold tight,' man. I told you."

"How long will it take, do you think? If I order them?"

"They're 80 bucks a piece. Probably take a week to get here." Gressley shakes his head. "You want to use my computer to order it? Maybe they'd pay you back?"

I stand still and think.

Gressley is back to his typing. "I don't blame you. I wouldn't trust those guys to pay up. Just not a priority. And anyway you're not getting them today."

"Security is the priority. Safety. That's my—"

"So we could shut down the station and strand all these people...." He looks across the station. There's no one here yet. "Or you could strip search them all."

"Shut up." I'm getting fed up with this kid. "Just shut up."

He smirks.

"I'm not strip searching anyone, you little pervert." I try to flip the batteries, but they only fit the one way. "You'd like that."

"Well, you can't shut down the station."

"Damn." I shake the wand again.

"Why don't you fake it?"

I've thought of this. It's pulsing in my throat.

"Pretend the damn thing is working and shut up about it."

"And you are the goddamn cynical lying future of the goddamn country!"

"Goddamn right!" He's back to his video game. "Break a leg, Hank!"

"Asshole."

I keep puttering, see if I can't squeeze out a flash or a buzz or I don't know what.

That bus will be here in forty minutes. Passengers will start arriving in twenty. There's no use rooting through the toilet paper again.

I slip the old batteries back in and shake it good. It won't work.

I'll fake it. It's just—

Clutter

terrorists, bombs, heart attacks, car wrecks, public speaking, beautiful women who aren't my wife, people speaking in languages I don't understand

The Wand

Squinting my eyes, willing the wand to buzz. I feel a throbbing in my throat.

Bus Station

The passengers line up outside my table-fence. A middle-aged woman, lipstick running up the cracks into her cheeks, and two young guys.

I poke through the woman's purse with my wooden stick—a reliable piece of equipment. Nothing unusual in the purse, but she's faintly embarrassed by it. Her other bag is a soft quilted thing. Instead of dumping it, I fondle the underside, find a hair brush, perhaps a curling iron. Ah yes, there's the cord.

"That's fine," I say. "Now please stand straight with your arms out." I lift the wand, then lower it. "All the change out of your pockets?"

I wave the wand slowly over her. Women are easy because they keep their keys in their purses. It's only jewelry sometimes, or a watch. When I reach the watch, I emit a sharp sound, electronic, from my throat. The volume surprises me, but I keep my mouth closed, my face calm.

"All right, Ma'am. You have a nice trip." I motion her past the barrier.

That wasn't so bad.

One of the men has only a duffel bag that I can poke at effectively enough, and no metal on his person except a wad of keys that he drops on the table. But the other fellow rolls a hard suitcase that I have to rifle through. The two men are together, and they are both nervous, so I am too. The first waits for the second, uneasily, shifting heel to heel, looking around.

I don't want to find drugs. I'm not authorized to deal with them, and it's embarrassing to let people see that. Fortunately—with some luck and some clever technique—I don't find any.

Next I have the man put his arms out so I can wand him. A dense, high-pitched beep emerges from my throat when the wand nears his waist. "Pockets?" I say.

He turns them out. Empty.

"Oh, probably your belt buckle."

He lifts his shirt, and there is no belt. He's standing stiffly now. The bright collar of his shirt is fussed underneath his jacket, but his shoulders are square. Maybe he wants to bully. After all, he's gotten the drugs by me.

I make a show of studying the wand. This kid can't get me. I won't let him. I hit the switch off and on. I hold it to my ear and shake it lightly.

"Let's try again." I wave the wand near his crotch and up. I guide it closer. Flinch just to see if he will. My throat constricts—it wants to beep, oh it wants to. But I hold it in. "Just a malfunction, I guess. You have a nice trip now." I wave the wand like a beacon, directing him to the benches beyond my checkpoint.

I catch a glimpse of Gressley, head in his hand, low behind the computer monitor. He's almost choking, he's laughing so hard. Asshole. I got them through on time, didn't I?

Clutter

lipsticks are the ones in the tubes and then those plastic cases falling open, leaking powders, perfume, brushes, combs, nail polish with a tiny brush inside each vial, razors, foam spurting out of aerosol cans and making creamy soup with the rouges powdering down the sides of the bag, fingernail clippers, nail files, cotton balls, cracked slivers of silver mirror glass

No knives are allowed inside the bus, but it's okay to pack them in the bags that go underneath. I ask which is which when I search them.

black bananas, fruit flies, lice, bedbugs, fleas

We don't ban the infested.

We never buy any hygiene items ourselves, Rosie and me. That's because Rosie brings home all those mini bottles from her hotel. The individually wrapped shaving razors, the shampoo, the single-thread sewing kits.

Rosie

Rosie is sympathetic about the batteries, but not too much. "Order them, Hank. I'm sure Phil will pay us back." She's changing out of her work clothes.

"It shouldn't come out of his pocket either."

"Hank, it won't." Now she's in the bathroom, but the door's open. She's about to peel the makeup off her face. It will come off in bright-colored swaths. Or maybe in layers. How much color can wash down a drain?

"And in the meantime?" I ask.

"We can afford—"

"—I mean the job. The security. The people on the bus!"

"Go up and down!" She's grinning in the mirror, half pale, half bright red. But I'm not in the mood for songs. Thank goodness that color washes down the drain.

"Rosie!" I snap.

"—It'll be fine, Hank!" Her tone is sharper now. "You faked it today, you can fake it tomorrow!"

"Bombs! Guns! Boxcutters!" The bed is quaking underneath me.

"Hank, this is Botkins, Indiana, we're talking about. The middle of fucking nowhere."

"It's lying."

"Come on, Hank. Everybody fakes a little bit."

"Not me."

She looks at me in the mirror. "It's only for a little while." Then her head is down over the sink again. Her face sputters into her hands, which are filling with water from the gushing faucet.

"I'd like to know if it doesn't matter, why I even go."
I don't think she hears me because I've said it softly.

But Rosie's shoulders tighten. "Do you want to quit?"

"I guess not."

Clutter

steak knives, bread knives, hunting knives, pocket knives, exactos, scissors

Rosie and me, we use hotel towels and don't even wash them. She hauls them back to the hotel and brings fresh ones. Same with the sheets and the pillowcases.

Rosie makes a tight bed—but she grumbles at it now, like she never used to.

It's a perk. The fresh laundry and the mini bottles. Rosie says so, and I don't believe she'd steal. Anyway, it's been thirty-five years of it.

bombs, knives, running out of space, suffocation, strangers

Bus Station

When I get to the station in the morning, I flip my tables same as always, line up the flat edges to be even with the floor tiles. Then I unlock the supply closet to find my stick and my wand. Of course the wand won't work, but there's a tingle when I pick it up, all the same. I run it along the outside edges of Gressley's ticket window—he's not here yet—and I'm sure there are no bombs there, no weapons stashed by him or anybody else.

Before too long, the passengers start to arrive.

This woman, is there violence in her? I focus, try to feel. But maybe I can't tell. I rummage through her bag, careful not to cut my fingers, but when I find the knives, they are cooking knives. They are safe in little plastic shields. "You have to keep this bag underneath, okay?"

She eyes me but nods, pulls the strap over her shoulder, and sits by the gate.

Factory

I miss the plant sometimes. The even spread of the line, the space between.

Clutter

Before I got to them, Rosie had a dozen bottles of pink fingernail polish and then another dozen or so of red. All of them less than a quarter left. You could hardly reach the paint in there with the tiny brush. It took a whole afternoon to combine the pinks and then the reds. I knew enough not to mix the two.

FastDog bus service doesn't have an official policy against wrapped presents, but how can I search them without ruining the paper? So I ask the passenger what it is and then warn them they should wait, next time, to do the wrapping.

Midwest, small towns, bus routes? People like me. Worth a bomb?

Rosie

Rosie appreciated my efforts, I thought.

But then, nearly a year ago, I learned she didn't.

"Were you digging around in here?" Rosie was poking through her jewelry box, which gaped open on her dresser. One hand reached far into a drawer, and the other cupped something tiny, palm up and fingers closed.

"I cleaned it yesterday," I said.

"You didn't throw anything away, did you?"

"Just duplicates."

"Duplicates of what?"

Necklaces hung from little hooks, sparkling and untangled. Rows of earrings lay gently across miniature satin pillows. "I made it neat for you."

"What did you throw out?"

"Mostly I untangled and cleaned—"

"—What did you throw out?"

"A plain necklace—like that one. And some earrings."

"The pearls?" Rosie picked up each earring, held it close to her eyes, and then dropped it into her cupped left hand. She must not have had her contacts in.

"Yeah, I kept one pair."

"Which pair?"

"Those. I threw away the old ones."

Rosie thumped her fist on the dresser. A flash of jewelry bounced from it, scattered over the surface and into her open underwear drawer.

"Were those expensive?" I asked.

"They were my mother's." A ring was still rolling in

looser and looser coils on the dresser top.

"I'm really sorry."

She breathed in deeply. "In the trash?"

"Pickup was this morning. That trash is gone."

She sat heavily on the unmade bed.

"I'm sorry."

"I know you are." She swatted at the bed covers, smoothed them uselessly.

"I didn't mean—"

"I know. I know. Just drop it. It's done."

"I'm sorry, okay."

"Jesus Christ, I don't care!" She tugged at the sheet beneath her, hopped her butt up from the bed, then back down. "I'm not mad." She stood then, pulled the sheet in a sweeping arc. "Can you leave me alone for a minute?"

I checked the trash, then took a walk under the open sky. When I came back, I stayed in the living room, alone.

A few weeks later, I started at FastDog.

Clutter

So I don't touch Rosie's dresser, even though it's a mess again.

A mess of dust and crumpled paper, price tags cut from clothing, earring backs, powder brushes, Rosie's long, stray, curling, waving hairs.

There's gray area, too. Like sports equipment. A baseball bat—does it count as a weapon?

The bombs, the killing, the terror. It's where you least expect it.

Bus Station

A few minutes after the woman with the cooking knives, there's a kid who has bottle rockets. I feel it.

"I'll be keeping these," I say, when I finally find the package tucked inside a pair of socks. "Any more in here?"

"No." He claps a hand to his pocket.

I figure there's another package, but when I wand him, my throat beeps, and it's a pocket knife. This kid is no boy scout. I take the knife and issue a pickup ticket.

"But I'm not coming back!"

"Should I give it to charity then?" I don't really have the authority to take things.

"Unh." This kid doesn't know that.

And he shouldn't be running around with knives! On a bus full of people!

The rest of the folks for Muncie have car keys and belt buckles, watches and coins. There's metal in the heels of their shoes, the spines of their suitcases. Gressley nods at me once or twice, even though his mouth is twisted and it's a begrudging sort of nod. Dayton comes next, and it's the same. Grand Rapids even later. More keys, more change, more boot heels.

My throat swells. But I don't find any weapons. I am watchful.

Clutter

shampoo, sewing kit, towels, sheets, pillowcases, bathrobes, toilet cleaner, Windex, toothbrushes, vacuum cleaner with extension for drapes and upholstery

It's stealing, after all. Rosie pocketing the soaps, the lotions, the laundry service.

Rosie

A few days after the wand dies, Phil has dinner at our house. He asks for more pork roast. I hold up my plate, too, and Rosie picks out a bit for each of us. Eating makes me quiet, but Rosie and her nephew chatter about his girlfriends and his softball team, and they each talk about their jobs. They tell each other about my work at the station.

"Hank had quite the challenge this week," Rosie says.

"Yes, the batteries," Phil answers. "But I believe the bus still ran on time!"

They both chuckle, and I don't add anything.

I haven't ordered the batteries yet. Phil told Rosie I could go ahead. But I didn't hear him say it. I don't trust him to pay up. Anyway, electricity is just more junk.

After Phil leaves, Rosie is rinsing dishes, then handing them to me, one after another, to cram in the dishwasher. Rosie won't let us have pie on top of where our meat sat. She brings out a whole new plate. We used to have nine big plates and eleven small ones, but I brought us down to four of each, for company.

When we finish the dishes, Rosie gets her purse and pulls out an envelope with a bunch of bills in it. "Phil brought that money for the batteries. Do you want me to put it in the bank?"

"Yes."

Rosie puts the envelope back in her purse. "I'm sure those batteries will get here soon."

Clutter

Rosie told me the Queen of England has nothing in her purse. She read it somewhere. But a homeless woman needs a whole shopping cart, at least on TV.

Newspaper says the plant is running more parts again. That's good for the crew. But more parts! I can't believe I contributed to that. Slow times cycle, of course. If it weren't for FastDog, maybe I'd go back. Maybe to parts...parts...parts...parts....

The favor to Phil is really to Rosie. I'm trying to make up for those earrings.

Bus Station

The next day is the same, mostly. It's so many people and so much stuff. A wand that won't light up, but my throat will. It burns with it.

I find a money clip deep in a man's jeans pocket. Then I wand folks good enough to empty their pockets, to keep their keys in their purses, who take off their shoes before I ask.

There's a college kid heading to Dayton. There's something about him, and I hassle him pretty good, flip his stuff like confetti. He's hiding something, defensive-like and squirmy. But I can't find it.

"I'm sorry, sir." The kid speaks in a quiet voice, but sarcastic. "Is there something you're looking for?"

I'm washing my hands in his clothes, elbow deep.

"Hands out," I say. He slumps his shoulders but holds up his hands. I wand him slowly, then shake my head. "You can go now."

"Is that wand even real?" He steps toward me. "It's ancient."

"You can go now."

"Beep," he squeaks as he re-zips his suitcase, catches a bit of cloth. "Beep." Then he pulls the zipper back, tries again. "Beeeeeeeeep."

Open Space

In the afternoon, I take a drive. These county line roads—they only exist to put the line on the map. I drive far from any houses, any people. I pull off, get out of the car.

The fields are brown, striped with windblown snow in the furrows. A distant row of trees breaks the plane, marking an old fence line between fields. The trees are stark black sticks, rooting upwards. The sky is the palest, coldest blue.

I squint to the horizon where the sky films up from the field. There's no rise in the ground, no swell. Flatness expands to every edge, past where my eyes can see.

I breathe in, and my lungs expand. Something snaps out through my chest—pops, cracks—like a silk parachute. A cold wind is filling me with air, but it's not wind or air—it's just space. There's room to breathe and breathe and breathe. I'm heady with it. I swell outward, to the clouds, to the edges of the sky, and then past those edges.

I stand until it scares me, the wild, free beauty of it.

By degrees, I pull myself back. I cram myself inside the car. I jingle my keys in the ignition and rumble away over the gravel that spits and scatters from the tires.

The Wand

Rosie didn't get that money from Phil. I don't know why, but she's lying to me. And I'm not going to spend my own money on batteries. Not when I can feel the metal.

Rosie

A long time ago, Rosie and I were young and lying tangled together, after sex, in one of the rooms she cleaned. She kicked at the sheets, which were wadded at the bottom of the bed, her legs still wrapped around mine. The bed rose and fell with our breathing.

Then Rosie sprung up and took hold of my ankle. She pulled.

"Hey!"

"Get off the bed. I want to show you something." She pulled harder, and my butt thumped to the floor.

"Rosie!"

"See what I do?" She pulled off the bed clothes, grabbed new from her cart and made the bed, tucked the sheets, crisp and clean and tight.

Rosie glowed, and I didn't know if it was pride in her bed-making or the love we'd just made. "See how quick I am? You should have timed me." She flopped, naked, onto the bed, bounced like a coin. "It makes my arms so strong."

"Come here." I pulled her off the bed, down to where I sat on the floor, and rubbed her muscled arms. "This is what I do at the plant." I was working on rotators then, so I guided her hands in a familiar clamp-tightening motion. The part I set every day, tightened just so, over and over.

She wriggled into me, less interested in the clamp than in restarting the love, but I was done for that session. When she saw that, she rolled out of my arms before I could finish the secret movements.

"Don't you want to see what I do?"

"I can't see it."

"Here." I took her arms again, worked the motions into her muscles, and she tried to pay attention. Of course, I didn't have the rotator or the stoppel or the bit. Rosie stopped wriggling and tried so hard, I could tell, to be impressed and proud of me. It was wavering in the air like a sheen between us. Maybe it was easy to let her fool me.

But when I switched to activators afterward, and then to clamps and on to neutralizators, I didn't tell Rosie. Couldn't bear to update the demonstration.

It was after I'd already switched that Rosie made a joke of the motion at the dinner table. It was funny, too. "Oh all day long you're playing." And she did it low, like it was dirty. It became a quiet joke, a signal for sex and sexiness. Then it grew into a sort of hand motion for hard work. I liked that, too. Now it means something else, like a shrug or an eyeroll, even though the motion is still that other thing. It just means, "Whatever you say."

Clutter

getting old, never having kids, overpopulation, losing your job, debt, hate, greed, lust, drugs, divorce, war, sadness

shampoo, soap, lotion, razors, laundry service, sewing kits, hairdryer, ketchup and mustard, coffee, curtains

I don't know if I'd go back to the plant, if I could.

Rosie and I don't have all that much sex anymore. But the potential is there. If I believe it might happen, well then it really might.

Bus Station

It's the next week, and Gressley is hammering the keyboard. "You finally got those batteries, huh?"

"What makes you think that?" Nothing has changed. The beep is still swelling from my body, not from the wand. And he's seen me do it. Every time, he watches me and smirks.

He leans up into the window. "I mean, I'm glad you fooled all those guys, but you couldn't have kept it up, right?"

"I suppose not."

His eyes flick from one of mine to the other. "No offense. You're not much of an actor."

"It's a relief, all right."

Clutter

napkins, coffee cups, mittens, pens, blankets, kitty litter, spare tire, floor mats of the same damn material as the floor anyway

Not in my car!

How much of life is faking it? Is anything real? Does it even matter?

Airport

With a whole afternoon to myself, I take a drive. Nobody on these roads and something satisfying about driving down the middle. The highway curls from my tires. I don't want to see the old Freiburger land. I can't stomach it. Instead, I drive to the airport, near where Rosie works. I leave the car in the drop-off line where the sign says not to, but I don't see why not.

Through the automatic doors, the room opens up over my head. The walls are white, and the carpet is patterned with toy airplanes. Behind a roped-off section, there are twenty seats and doors labeled "Gate 1" and "Gate 2." I don't try to get through—I respect security barriers—but find a place against the wall.

A family is passing through the checkpoint. The mother places her shoes, her purse, her daughter's shoes, into a plastic tub. The dad empties his pockets—keys, change, red and white peppermints crumbling out of clear film. He slides his belt off like drawing a sword.

Instead of rifling through the bags, these guards—three!—send them through an x-ray machine on a conveyor belt. Slinking sideways along the wall, I get a better angle on the screen. Personal items appear in comic-strip colors. Rattling bottles, a hair dryer with a tangled cord. One at a time, the mom, dad, and daughter step through the metal detector partitions. Another guard holds a wand but doesn't use it. It is small and sleek. Shinier than mine, with more parts that glow.

A different guard checks the big suitcases. He swipes them with these slips of powdery paper.

"Hey, there." I step behind the guard, who is leaning into an open suitcase. "What's that powder stuff do? Clean the shine from your nose?"

"It checks for explosives."

There's a little boy watching, too. He asks, "How *does* it work?"

"I can't give away my secrets." The guard chuckles.

"Oh, c'mon!" the boy says. But his parents are calling, and he springs away.

"Yeah. C'mon." I give a chuckle, too. "How does it work?"

The guard's hands are back in the suitcase, but his head turns at the neck. "Sir, do you have a bag to check?"

"I was just watching."

"Do you have a *reason* to be here?"

The man's uniform is dark and crisp. I go.

Rosie

I tell Rosie about the guard and what he said to me, but I say it tough, like it's not a big deal. "Asshole," I say. "Don't you think?"

Rosie is digging through her purse. She's sitting at the kitchen table, so I only see her arms and shoulders and head. "You should hear what a woman said to me today. She wasn't from around here."

"Come to think of it, this fellow had a snooty accent, too."

"My woman called me *Sweetheart*—she said it very sarcastic." Rosie dumps her bag on the table. "And she didn't like the light switches! C'mon, the light switches? I was pleasant to her later all the same, but she had nothing to say to me."

"Doesn't take much to be friendly," I say.

"Couldn't they at least pretend?" She must be looking for aspirin because when she finds the bottle, she takes one. Then she leaves the mess on the table and charges out of the room.

Clutter

It's pens and coins and lint and gum and lipstick. A small comb, a button, nail file, a broken off pencil eraser.

canes, baseball bats, pearl earrings, batteries, Rose's stealing, bottles and bottles and bottles

How will we find the terrorists?

loose change, strangers, death

It's just with so many and so much. No order and just clutter.

The Wand

I'm not controlling the throat beeps any more, if I ever was. They glow from my voice box. I can't prove it, but I know they're dead right.

Bus Station

The next day, like usual, I am the first one at the bus station. My boots echo on the tiles. When I get the wand from the closet, I slap it against my hand, tap it on the walls. The station is smaller than the airport, much smaller. Still, before the people come, there's room, at least, to breathe.

But then they trickle in. Gressley to type at his computer. Four passengers to Muncie, then gone, six to Dayton and their crumbs on the floor that I scoop up. Gressley hasn't sold any tickets for Grand Rapids, and he leaves before the bus comes. But there's internet tickets, so I stay. Just in case.

And then there he is, one passenger. He's a skeptic. I can read it on his face, in the way he holds his shoulders, twists his neck. When he opens his suitcase, I poke through everything he distrusts: the bus schedule, the wand, the government, the security guard right in front of him. I rattle his laptop carrier. Then I swipe over him with my wooden stick. Oh! Well, he makes me nervous. I switch the stick for the wand while his jaw loosens and the slack of his mouth quivers. The wand and my throat find the keys in his pocket. Beep.

He throws them on the table. "Aw, you got me."

And now he'll sit with his paranoia. His mind all cluttered with conspiracy. He can't live like this, pretending it's all okay.

Rosie

When the last bus has gone, I don't lock the wand away. Not this time. I take it home.

Because I have to show Rosie. I have to let her know that I'm not a fake. Because it's real. It's real. I promise it's real.

There she is, half-dressed in the bedroom, stripped of her makeup, the pins in her hair. Her polyester uniform pants are still on, frayed hem draping over pink toenails. She's unfastening her bra, twisting her arms behind her, elbows pointed into wings.

I step behind her, release the clasp. She lets me lower her to the bed.

"Do you want to see what I do at work?" I ask.

"Are you going to strip search me?"

"Oh, it's worse than that."

She giggles, bucks up, reaches for the wand. "What are you doing?"

I kneel on the bed beside her, then straddle her. I run my metal detecting wand, powerless, in a straight line over her body. Her arms and their freckles. Down the softness of her torso, between both our legs, all the way to her pink-polished toenails.

And because I'm not a fake, I can feel the metal in my throat, feel the metal in Rosie. I can find it. It's a beep that swells, then bubbles out.

It's too much. It's too much.

Open Space

Late at night, when Rosie is asleep, I throw my covers off. I go behind my house, still naked, put the small cluster of a town behind me, and look outward, into the open night. Stars sprinkle the top layer, crowded but too far away to touch me. And underneath is sweeping darkness, flat and smooth. Empty fields stretching to the horizon. Wide open. I feel me some space.

Then I feel a little better, but I still can't sleep, so I go back inside. I find a project to keep me busy.

The Mole

You are at the doctor's office to have a mole removed. You are surprised to be there. You think, what a waste of time!

The mole is dark brown and has been on your arm for as long as you can remember. A single dark hair springs from it. You've forgotten to pluck it, and so you pull at the hair with your fingers, but you can't grip it. The mole is ugly, but not memorable. It is round and flat like a dime.

The doctor passes a finger over the mole. "You say it's grown?"

"Well, no," you say. "I don't think so."

This doctor is not your regular one. She fingers it again, less gently. "I agree that we should remove it." She lays out a sharp line of shiny instruments.

The doctor pokes the tip of a small syringe into the skin just under the mole—before you've braced yourself. But it doesn't hurt, not much. She pulls the syringe out, moves it a millimeter, and pokes again. She pierces the skin at the edge of the mole and slides the needle beneath it. Then she does it again. Each time the doctor pulls her needle from your arm, a white swell of skin bubbles in its place. The white skin lifts the dark mole, which has also begun to balloon. As the doctor drills the tiny syringe around the outside edge of the mole, the mole bulges like a water blister, larger and larger. It reminds you of mayonnaise squishing out of a hamburger bun. You shudder, but only slightly. You tense your shoulders. You hold your arm very still.

The doctor places the small syringe on the table and picks up a razor. It's a curved piece of metal that she holds with her thumb on one end and her finger on the other. It looks springy, and the sharpness pulses outward to bend in a simple, graceful arc. The doctor eases the razor beneath the swollen mole, and then she saws—gently, gradually, grotesquely—to expose a blotch of gooey redness. It's too red, too gooey. The last edge of the mole clings to your forearm, and the doctor slices—it breaks free! The cut smarts, but not much. It isn't so bad.

The only strange thing is you are smaller. But that makes sense. A part of you has been cut off, so you should be smaller.

Except. You really do feel smaller. You feel much smaller. Way too small.

You think to make a joke to the doctor—what joke?—about feeling so small. She will reassure you. But when you try to say it, you can't speak. You can't open your mouth. You have no mouth, no throat, no tongue. It has all been cut away. By the razor! How can that be?

You must show the doctor. Where *is* the doctor? You try to look, but your eyes are gone. And your ears! Cut away. Cut away.

Panic seizes you, and it seems as though your arms and legs will flail violently. But they are gone, too.

You can't breathe—you have no lungs—you can't scream.

There is nothing. There is nothing.

And then a tingly, horrible knowing washes over you. At least, it washes over the small part of you that is left.

Somehow that part of you that thinks, that feels, that is (Is it a soul? You've never been religious…), it has not clung to the larger part of your body, not to the head and heart and hands. Instead, it has lodged itself in the other part, the part meant to be discarded.

You are the mole.

Curse the Toad

When I see the toad, just *staring* at me, I scoop him up, flip my skirt around my shoulders, and wedge the toad into the slit between my legs. I guess I'm curious.

The toad doesn't die. He flips right out and comes up sputtering. But when he settles down, he stays on the forest path. He stares.

I don't have time for the nonsense. I smooth the skirt down and to the house I go. The cottage where I live and also where I brew things and such.

The toad follows.

Must not be one of my guys after all. They'd know better.

I go about my business. I skin and clean the rabbit that's strung on the hook in the shed, roast the loin for supper, then grind and spice the rest for sausage. Not much in this world is tastier than rabbit sausage.

As the loin cooks, the toad hops up the stone steps, right through my open door. The same toad.

Maybe it *is* one of mine. Maybe it *liked* the humiliation. Maybe a good sniff of the witch that cursed him...well, maybe he can't get enough.

Pervert.

He keeps watching me, but I ignore him.

I eat the roasted rabbit loin with a salad of tough greens from the garden. A splash of lemon would brighten the salad, but of course there is none to be had.

Lemons! Why do I think of such things? I used to buy citrus from the boy at the docks, but where did he go? Now the dockworkers only watch me when I come alone, curses hissing under their breath or mine.

Still, I clean my plate, sopping jus and vinegar with a slice of good bread. I almost lick the plate, but there is the toad, a judgment. I won't teach him manners or feed him, either.

I wipe away the last grease of it, the dishtowel thick with suds.

In the morning, the toad is in a different corner, his mouth downturned, as I throw water on my face and tug a comb through snarled hair. I don't often bother, but now, with this odd guest. Well.

Breakfast is porridge. Stirred and stirred until my arm aches with the motion and with the rain that's coming, but it's worth every stroke. Some honey. And cream from the goat.

Not a bit left over for the toad.

I don't know which one of them he once was. His mouth turns down, his skin so mottled. Not that dock boy, with his grin and light hair that lifted. But how could I remember them all?

He's watching me still, after breakfast and all day. The toad. Crouched in the corner, his eyes follow me, or maybe they don't, as I feed carrots and onions to the stew pot on the fire. I stir. He croaks.

Boys and men, rambling through my garden, pulling rabbits from my woods, plucking daisies for their sweethearts. They call me "Bony Knees" or "Old Fuzzy." What do they want, when they do that, but to be toads?

He jumps at mid-day, hops closer to the fire, and I think he'll hop right in. Careless toad.

So I poke him back with the wooden spoon. I don't much like touching, though his skin is soft like suede. An unlikely feel, it lingers on my palm and tingles, still, between my legs. His look lingers, too, and I wonder what he's thinking. He sees the mud on my floor and how the sunshine floats the dust and the shimmery cobwebs. It was yesterday when I held him to me, in the woods.

Later, when I weed the garden, hacking the thistles from among the turnips, I'm bent so I do look old, I suppose, over this hoe.

"Mrs. Elbow," one called me. I know how he got the elbow part. I'm all elbows in my cloak that drapes like a tablecloth. Just skinny points sticking out the corners. But "Mrs."? Was he mocking me, that one? He got what he deserved.

The next morning, it's forest trails and foraging, the sun too bright for spell books. Back at the cottage, there's nothing to do in the garden but pick a few bright peppers. Shall I munch them, raw and fiery? Or dice them up and into the stew?

In the afternoon, the goat is loose again. She pulls her peg and off she goes. But I know where—through the woods. There she is, nibbling. I prod my pocket for the bread crust, the bait to pull her back, and what do I find but the toad? He springs from my pocket to the leaf-covered ground. Go away now, toad.

It's not that they have anything better to call me. "Miss" or "Ma'am," though I crave it.... It wouldn't sound right, not through those fleshy lips. Not aimed at me, the crone, living lonesome in these woods. Even the boy with the fruit, the salt breeze, and a polite question about home, his family that wasn't there or any for me either. He never said it.

Why do I think of him? I squint at the toad, who's followed me back to the house yet again.

The fire is hot, but I poke it hotter. Too hot for the weather but not for the stew, and my sweat is running, bubbling out beneath my skirts and the shirt that is rolled and tucked. Curse the toad—he's watching, and I won't strip further.

I'm not even a crone yet, though they don't know it. Or maybe they do. Maybe it's the smell of blood that draws them.

I've turned the magic into other things. Like the men into toads.

I've had no children, past the one. Her arms were wings, her legs were claws. Her hair was thin and fine, like feathers when the breeze lifted it. She'd have been a wonder if she'd only learned to breathe.

Or maybe she wasn't a she. I couldn't know before I buried her. Poor thing.

And so the magic. Who can blame me? Who but the boys, the men, the toads?

The toad won't make a noise, not a croak or a hiss. Not today, it seems. But his throat swells again and again, shrinking between swells to nothing. My own breath slows to match his.

They don't know my name. Too much power to be lost in giving it, can you blame me?

I shouldn't have kissed him, not with those lips, too powerful. I never learn. Never learn to be careful of the magic.

I poke the fire, then the stew. This pot's only dinner.

The toad is still with me. His eyes peer out but from the other corner now. He doesn't even blink.

Why am I so certain he's a he? No way to tell, not that I know. All toads, like all men and boys, they look alike.

Only wings and claws make a difference. But breathing, too. What about the breath?

Did he steal a peach—this toad, this man, this boy? Ripe and fuzzy? Juice oozing down his shirt and through his fingers? Well, how did it taste, little toady? Was it better than the bugs you eat now?

In the morning, I wake to a stench, and I can't breathe, not well. It's rotting rabbit. I pry apart the meat grinder. Before drawing water for myself, for my face and my porridge, I draw it for this. Rinse out the rotten scraps from sausage making. It's the toad's fault that I forgot, that I left it screwed to the table to rot and to stink for days with tiny bits of heart and ear and liver.

His stare—it isn't accusing like I thought, not angry. I think he pities me, the monster. How dare he?

I rub petals on the table—hyacinth and primrose. Scatter them through the room to mask the smell. I rub them on my arms and legs. Crush them between fingers black from the rich dirt of my garden.

I haven't seen him eat a bug. Not a bread crumb, either. Does he eat? Is he trapped here, enchanted by my smell, my spells, or by the memory of my smell? Can he smell? Why won't he leave? Why won't he hop away to eat some bug or other food? Must I feed him? I can't be responsible. I can't be blamed.

The sun is down, and the fire is low. I quench my last candle.

Then I sit up in bed and search for the glow of his eyes. I look, I really look, but I can't find them. Leaves rustle outside the window, and the black of inside is darker than it must be out there, under the sky. The wind quiets, and the silence is deeper now, without the toad.

It's like their silence then, about the baby, the wings and the claws. The people at the market wouldn't speak, wouldn't look at me. The smell of lemons and the empty basket. My shawl tight around a belly still pouched, and the boy with the sharp eyes. Only he looked, to judge or to pity, and to see.

The sun rises. The toad is on my chest, a soft weight, when the sun shines in and wakes me. He doesn't blink, but the pulsing of his throat is like blinking. It swells, and then it shrinks. His skin is thick and bumpy when I touch it. Yet it's so delicate. If only—if he didn't breathe so softly. If he didn't *stare* at me like that.

I pick him up, cradle him in two hands. There's magic, I remember it now, magic in my other lips. The softness of them. Between my legs is a different kind.

I bring him to my face, so close that my eyes lose focus and he's fuzzy. Not a toad at all, but a patch of soft green. He could be anybody.

A kiss, so quick, and he's fumbling, naked in my bed. A full grown man, pink-skinned beneath the wiry hair. He's tangled in sheets and in my limbs. I jump up, untangle, while he thrashes.

I thought I'd know his face. I thought I'd know it.

The creature finds his feet, finally, crashes into the stew pot with a hiss that slops stew on the floor and a bright welt of burn into his thigh. Then he's out the door and running, naked, into the woods.

Maybe he wasn't one of mine, after all. Maybe I've just cursed a toad to become a man.

"Beth!" I call after him. "My name is Beth."

Boobman

Monday

So let's get the big question out of the way right off. This story is about that guy. The one you see riding through town on a bike, all in spandex, with a poufy blonde wig and boobs like helium balloons. That's Mike Chesterton.

Why does he do it? Because he feels like it. It's just what he does.

He's also an electrician. It's the perfect job for him. Long, impossible days, often tedious, tracing wire to wire to wire. But there's glory in it, too. Just think: he takes a dark house and lights it up. Some day he'll get an emergency call, he knows he will, in the middle of the night—then he'll be a real hero. In the meantime, it's good money.

What does his wife think about his hobby? The boobs? The bike? She thinks he's a little odd, but it's not a big deal. Patty does some strange things, too. Like reading the newspaper in alphabetical order. Like running her flip-flops through the dishwasher.

Just about every evening, after work, Mike drives to the park and hides the car behind some trees. Then he slips into the public restroom to strap on his gear. He pops the boobs into orbit with a shoulder twitch and a pelvic wiggle. The wig whispers into place, and he clamps it with bobby pins. Spandex hugs his thighs, tickles his chest, statics up his backside. He swings the bike from the trunk, and he's off. The best part of his day.

Today he's spinning, as usual, over the asphalt jogging path, bike zipping underneath him, twisting at the pavement. He pumps his legs, the balloons in front of him bumping up and down, one and the other. A shift in his hips and the whole pattern changes. They bump together and apart. Thighs burn, vibrations juice through him. The wind whips at him, tickling his torso.

Trees and flowers and mothers with strollers all warp into bright and unusual shapes. The landscape on a bike. It's open air so he can really see. Mike looks sideways, and the colors smear as he passes. Skateboarders swoop then stretch out backward with his movement. Kids chase him, too, running or skating or pedaling bikes. Faces smirk, but it's clown smiles when he passes them, harmless. Even their words spiral.

Then the quick glimpses when he gets to the edge of the park where there are houses and backyards edging the path. Curtainless windows are like comic book panels, but he passes so quickly that the shapes warp there, too. A fraction of a second, a slice of a life. A woman on the couch. A man lunges at a dog. One child kicks another. Just a flash, a slap—he wonders if he really saw it. When he looks far away, the perspective changes. It's still and smooth. The trees line against the horizon. The playground slide is still against the sunset, sharp and straight in its stand-up form.

After a couple of circuits, Mike loops to the trees where he hid his car. There's something strange on the ground— glimmering, sparkling, flashing. He jerks to a stop, unclips his feet from the pedals, and dismounts.

His car's windshield is shattered. Smeared on the hood is "BOOBMAN" in neon pink spray paint.

For just a moment, Mike is pissed. Blood rises, and his fists clench and release. The clips of his shoes rattle faster against the pavement. But then he remembers being young. He touches paint that's still tacky, drags a toe through glass pebbles. The satisfaction that must come from smashing a windshield! The spark of pure joy in the thrust, the crack, the explosion. It's annoying. But the car is insured, and there's nothing inside kids would steal.

He changes into his day clothes, then calls a tow truck. He walks his bike home, lugs his toolbox and the gym bag of hair and boobs and spandex. His tools are heavy, and it's slow going, but the breeze is nice, and Mike thinks about the boobs bouncing above his bike tires. He remembers the elongated park shapes when he rides, how they stretch into meaning. And those bubbling, smearing letters stretched out across his car.

Boobman. He likes it. It's better than what else they call him. He's Boobman. Like a superhero or something.

When he finally makes it home, Patty is in the kitchen, running water over some frozen cube steak. "Where's the car?" she asks. Mike tells her about the windshield, and she pulls her hands up, bright pink from under the water. "Mike! Who would do that?"

"Some kids hang out there. I see their beer bottles and cigarette butts. Their comic books."

Patty pokes at a hangnail, thoughtfully. "Maybe you should change at home. It'd be safer."

"That wouldn't bother you?" Mike has always tried to keep his boobs out of the neighborhood so as not to embarrass his family. But maybe Patty's right. The kids are grown now and out of the house. He can bring this home.

What does it feel like? His bike in the wind? The orbs bouncing? The hair streaming? It's kind of like Superman, he supposes, when he's really flying.

Patty doesn't like to tell people what she does for a living, even though she's an accountant, a CPA. Mike doesn't know what's to be ashamed of in that. But it's the quirks that make him love her so much.

And Patty will slap him sometimes when she's in a particular mood. Flat, open hand on the ass or on the meaty part of his leg. She does it for the sound, she says. Mike loves the sound, too. It makes a nice smacking-sucking-reverbrating twang when she places it right.

Mike wouldn't change anything about Patty. He couldn't make her better than she is. Also, it's not his place to, not his business, if you really think about it.

Tuesday

Mike is at the front door of a new client, one Mr. Thomas Klacken who found his ad in the church bulletin and wants his basement wired. The door opens before Mike can ring the bell, and a tall man in a suit almost steps right into him. The man's shoulders twitch. Then he says, smooth as anything, "Talk to my wife," and glides past.

There's a bony, youngish woman in the front room, stooped, picking up bits of something from the carpet.

"Mrs. Klacken?" Mike keeps his hand in his pocket in case she doesn't want to shake it. "Mike Chesterton? Electrician?"

"Yes, I'm Melanie Klacken." She straightens, looks at something over Mike's shoulder, and then at him. She smiles, just barely.

She leads him down to the basement, which is half-finished, concrete floors and bare drywall slapped up in a hurry. Hanging above a washer and dryer is a single light bulb. There's nothing else. Mike follows her around the room to see the pencil marks her husband has made on the walls. Her feet are bare on the concrete floor and make a dry sound as she shuffles.

As Mike sets to work, Melanie Klacken seems antsy. She climbs up and down the stairs repeatedly, runs laundry up from the machine, offers him glasses of water. He can tell she doesn't trust him alone, but that's not unusual.

Eventually, she brings down that same basket of laundry and starts to fold it. He gets a look at the top of her head. Her white scalp is stark where the hair parts in a jagged line. She's got on smudgy makeup and sweatpants with a drawstring cinched tight so it hurts to look at her waist and the pinch of belly poking just over. When she leans to reach for a sock, her shirt slides up her back. There's something dark there, maybe a bruise or else a large birthmark snaking across her torso. She tucks the T-shirt into the sweatpants, forces it tighter against the drawstring.

"You seem familiar," she says.

"It's church. St. Chuck's. I've seen you there with your husband."

She holds a towel clamped at her chin, and her arms make big wings of it and flap them together. She looks at Mike again. "Sorry I didn't recognize you. We just moved here in March."

She goes upstairs then. Maybe she trusts him now.

It's good that she's gone because her husband's marks need adjusting. Mike puts his head down and gets at it. There's no reason he can't finish the job today. Pliers in the hole, needling, stitching, wrapping, whirling. Tight and shred it out in frazzled ribboning ends. Wire to wire to wire. Clamp and twist.

Mike is making good time until some peculiar ravel of wire winds through his fingers and into his brain. There's something vicious there that reminds him of his car, the windshield, the neon spray paint. Suddenly he's sure it was the kids who chase him. He feels their hot breath on his calves, hears the way they hoot slurs and obscenities. Mid-fish, he chokes. He can't get the thread through. Wire deadends in the wall with a rasping thud. His arms are scraping at the hole he's cut in the drywall. He's reaching further, up to his shoulder. The clean edge is crumbling. But fuck good form at this point. Fifth attempt now. Sweating, breathing hard. But if he changes clothes at home—Patty is right, it's safer. Or does the road make it worse? He only knows he can't give it up. His heart's going into a flutter-beat. He'll try once more, he decides, then finish this job up quick. So he pulls the fucker up, stretches his arms, and wiggles his fingers. He walks a lap around the basement before starting again. It finally fishes clean. He completes the rest of the project and gives a nod to Mrs. Klacken on the way out.

At home, it's a miracle of convenience. Mike can get dressed in his own room with space to spread out, no knocking against the tiny bathroom walls. And a clean mirror for fluffing the curls. Then it's exhilarating to emerge from his house, all dolled up, where the neighbors can see him. When he toe-walks down his driveway, he prances a little, click-click in his clip-in shoes. He's a whipped-up torrent of blonde feathering on top, round and wild and shoulder-width, then a bubble—two bubbles—of perfect, round, bouncing fullness. A quick taper to solid torso, narrow hips. His legs diminish to a point at his sharp-arched, extended feet. Then he hops on the bike, which neutralizes the streamlined shape of him, curls his back into a crouch.

Two turns through his subdivision and he's on Bruce Road, a twist of a thruway that he's never biked before. It's a three-mile stretch of asphalt, two lanes in each direction. It coils out of his neighborhood, then swings in a big looping curve, cutting through cornfields before wrapping itself to the park where the cars can't follow him. There's no sidewalk, just a grassy ditch on either side and an aluminum guardrail down the middle. It's a glorious stretch for a bike.

The fields are flat, but leaves roll in the wind, knee-high corn like an ocean. They're blurred at the edges where the sky hits the ground but fuzzy because of distance. The telephone poles, on the other hand, and the flowers in the ditches, those are blurred from movement, power lines coursing-swelling-stringing from Mike's pedaling through space.

Then into the park, and it's a perfect day for his bike. Except there's one odd shape that keeps appearing in his mind. Mrs. Klacken and that bruise, that flash of darkness, coiling up a bright white torso.

When the sky starts to color, it's time to head back. There isn't traffic on Bruce Road, so he lets go of the handles and spreads his arms. Thin wisps of air run through his fingers like electrical wires fizzing smoothly in sharp, tiny currents. Mike has a little bit of sixth sense in peddling his bike and running wires—he's not exactly psychic, but there's this feel to it, life stringing through him and connecting him to the world.

A car pops out of the horizon behind him and quickly catches up. The kids. They slow down to tail him closely, at least five packed into a station wagon, honking and screaming. Mike stays steady, that's the trick. He can't look sideways. Shit, on this road a wobble could kill him. They finally zip past.

He doesn't think the kids mean any harm. It's a joke to them. But he wishes they'd leave him alone.

You won't see Mike's boobs anywhere but his bike. He doesn't wear ball gowns or tutus, either. Never pantyhose or high heels. Only cycling gear. Only the hair, the breasts, the Spandex. A swipe of red lipstick. But only when he's riding.

He sometimes thinks about growing his fingernails out, how the wind would pull at them, creep underneath, tug him in one more way. But he keeps them short for Patty. Sex with Patty is gentle, painfully soft, and overflowing with sweetness. Claws would ruin that.

Are they really balloons, his boobs? Of course not. Balloons would pop too easy. Mike doesn't want an explosion out there, or even a slow leak.

After his ride, he showers and comes downstairs just as Patty throws her car keys on the kitchen table. Mike is shirtless, so she tweaks a nipple as she kisses him on the forehead and asks about his day.

"Patty, you know how I get feelings, how I run from wire to wire and know things that I don't have any business knowing?"

Patty is flipping through the mail. She throws up her arms, a bill clutched in each hand. "You're not psychic!"

"What about at the lake? With Kraussman's dog?"

"You've got good instincts." Patty opens a circular so it unfolds and blocks her body.

"Whatever you call it, you know I got it." Mike sits at the kitchen table and folds his bare arms in front of him.

"Maybe."

"Maybe?"

"Okay. You know things sometimes. You figure things out."

"Well, this asshole I just did a job for, I figured out he hits his wife."

"Oh, God. Is she okay?"

"She hides it. Won't talk about it or admit anything."

"So you don't know for sure."

"I'm sure."

"Well, if she doesn't say...." Patty frowns. "I don't see what anybody can do."

"I know. It's just a shame."

"I feel horrible for that woman," Patty says. Then she refolds the advertisement, stacks it with the other junk letters.

Patty doesn't mind the biking gear. Just like Mike doesn't mind her quirks. Patty, she talks to dinner sometimes. He walks in, and she's lecturing a pork chop or cheering on the mashed potatoes. "Little mini pizza," she says, "now why won't you slide off this cookie sheet and listen to me?"

Mostly, Mike and Patty don't talk about his habits. Because what is there to say? She'll sometimes offer advice out of the blue about how to tie back his hair, and when there's a sale on gear, or if the roads are slick with rain. But mostly she leaves him to himself about it.

Wednesday

Mike gets a call for a new subdivision, wiring bare rooms. It's easy work with the walls open. Usually his favorite thing, too. So clean with that space to work and nothing broken yet by amateurs or corroded by time. When he doesn't have to hack through drywall, when the lines are right at his fingers and he can follow them with his eyes, he thinks about the bike and the boobs, the joy of whizzing over smooth and twisty roads. But today it's the Klackens in his brain, too.

After work, he dresses and jumps straight on his bike. Colors are sharp, shapes are smearing gloriously. The air currents wrap around and underneath the balloons, spin off, cross at his breastbone. The wind sucks at his wig, tugs at the clips that hold it in place, and nestles between the nylon and his real, buzz-cut scalp. The air in his teeth feels like a toothpaste commercial.

Mike is shaped like a speeding bullet—pointed toes, tapered legs, then large and full up top. Or maybe he's an arrow, and his curls are the feather on the shaft.

He pedals hard and fast and takes the curve at a slant, the wind rustling up his bangs. On Bruce Road, he rides top speed. There's just a flash at the edge of his vision—a truckload of kids—that he feels more than sees.

These have been the same kids for thirty years, he thinks, haunting him on the roads and in the park. His nemeses, you might say. But he's sure they don't mean any harm.

He hears the yell, "There's the queer!" It's stretched out in the air, tickling just past his ear lobe and twisting up into the tendril that blows there. He slides to the shoulder but keeps his speed. The truck is approaching so fast. It screeches and swerves at his rear tire. It doesn't hit, but it's close. It should pass him now, but the truck slows to just his speed instead. He keeps exactly on the line, the edge of the asphalt, before the road drops into gravel, then ditch. The kids stay behind him. He catches a sharp flash of smile, maliciously stretched over open teeth.

Shit. He bails. He tips his bike off the road and barely keeps upright as he flies down the ditch and crashes at the bottom.

Mike is fortunate to be armored in padded boobs and a helmet of hairspray. His bike is fine. So he waits a minute, then straightens out his chest harness and pulls the bike up to the road, just as another car pulls onto the shoulder. It's Patty in the Taurus.

"Mike! Oh my god, what happened to you?"

Patty is out of the car and scrambling over the asphalt. Mike props himself on the bike, one foot half-clipped into a pedal.

Patty pulls something from his hair. "What is this?" It's grass. "And you're crooked." She tugs at his wig, one hand over each ear. "You were run off the road. Oh, my god, it was those kids. They passed me earlier, going way too fast." Patty's voice gets shrill. She jerks harder at Mike's wig. He loses balance and spikes his pedal foot at the ground, but Patty doesn't let go. "Are they the same ones? In the park, with the windshield? Jesus Christ, Mike! You're going to get yourself killed!"

"Can we talk about this later?" Mike clicks his foot back in place. "After my ride?"

There are tears bubbling in Patty's eyes, but not overflowing. "Will you please come home now?"

"Just a short ride. Once through the park."

"Mike, I want you to get in the car."

"Once through the park. Please? I need it."

"I want you to get in the car."

"Fuck, Patty. Fine. Open the goddamn trunk." He slams his bike in, slams the trunk, and then slams the passenger door after he climbs in. They don't talk the whole ride home. Mike just pulls off his wig and plays with the curls.

You know how you wear that little white skirt to play tennis? Or how you wrap that belt around yourself for karate class? It's the same thing with Mike and the boobs.

Patty hasn't forbidden his riding—not that she could stop him, if it came down to it—but he decides to give it a day before he goes back out. Just to respect her opinion.

Thursday

Another day of bare walls in the new housing, and

it's just wire to wire, making connections, no drywall to cut through or block his thoughts. Lines glow from his fingers, make shapes in his brain, and a dark bruise still spirals.

Mike is annoyed he can't ride the bike after work, but he won't break his promise. He checks the tire pressure instead, makes sure no bolts are rattling or too tight. He repairs his own bike when it needs it, but nothing is off today for him to fix.

So he takes a walk. The houses in his neighborhood look different at the slower pace. More square, the corners are sharper. Mike is watching shapes, winding through his neighborhood into the next. He doesn't know too many of these people, but folks seem respectable. Through the windows, he watches for the kids who chase him. Maybe they wear a different face when they do homework or eat dinner with their parents. Maybe they're not leering.

It's dark when Mike reaches the Klacken house. Their kitchen is lit, just the man and the woman sitting at the table with a casserole dish. The man slashes the air with his fork. The woman is still, but her eyes follow his hands. Mike isn't sure what to make of it.

When he gets home, he gives the bike a wash in the driveway, in the dark. Warm bucket of soapy water. He sudses the seat and handlebars, wipes the frame, scrubs the tires. Then a blast with the garden hose. Looking at the bike, hooking his thumbs in the spokes, and thinking about tomorrow, the shapes warping, and the wind, and his full bouncing breasts—it cheers him right up.

No, he doesn't shave his legs. He doesn't have to shave his chest or back either, in case you're wondering. Does he wear panties? Well, that's getting awfully personal, don't you think?

Friday

Back at the construction site, Mike has to clean up after another electrician, some apprentice who cut too short, and Mike pulls out so much wire and starts again. It feels good to set a thing right.

After work, Mike is feeling bold in his boobs. He pedals through the surrounding neighborhoods, lets himself be seen. He waits until it's almost dark to ride down the Klackens's street, waits until Mr. Klacken will be home from work. He slows when he reaches their block. It's harder to balance at that pace, and the boobs are swinging far to the left, then far to the right.

There are two silhouettes in the window. Then the man's arm lifts and moves so fast. The woman's head swings. Her hair flies.

But Mike is past too quickly to be sure. He circles the block and is approaching their house a second time when a car peels from their driveway. It's Mr. Klacken. Mike drops the bike on the lawn and click-clacks to the door, which opens as he gets there.

Melanie Klacken's head is down, her hair dragging in front of her eyes. "I'm glad you came back."

"Miss?" Mike shifts from one foot to the other.

She looks up then and gasps. "I thought you were—"

"It's Mike Chesterton, the electrician?" He pulls at his wig but only tugs it sideways. "Don't mind the...I saw... through the window...I thought you might need help."

"What did you see?" She looks past him at the street. "Oh god, come inside."

Mike steps into her living room. "It looked like—"

"—It's not what it looked like." She shuts the door behind him.

"Okay." Mike swipes his wrist across his mouth to wipe off some lipstick. He wiggles the wig harder, and when it finally peels loose, he pockets the clips and holds the curls in two hands.

"Oh god. Dinner." She moves through the living room to the kitchen, and Mike follows. His shorts are riding up, so he gives them a good yank when her back is turned. The boobs are still hovering nicely, floating front and center, juicy and round. With both hands he pulls down on them, hoping to smoosh them lower in his halter top, but there's no flattening these babies, no hiding who he is.

On the front burner of the stove, she's got a pot of water in a noisy boil. Behind it, there's what smells like tomato sauce. Her back is to Mike as she dumps a box of dry spaghetti noodles into the water. "Sorry," she says. "Thomas will want dinner when he gets home."

"Smells good."

She seems to be relaxing as the boil builds again in the pasta water. "What exactly did you see?"

"Not much, really." Mike's bike shoes click on the floor when he steps forward. "I just have a suspicion."

She mumbles "suspicion" in a low under-her-breath whisper. Her elbows press into her sides. She's got a big spoon in her hand, which she squeezes, then lays carefully on the counter. She pivots on one heel to face Mike again. "I'm sorry. Why are you here?"

He looks at her for a minute, building up his nerve. He's searching for a mark on her, something to steel him. Nothing on the arms or neck. Her legs are covered by jeans.

Then she looks right at his wrist, the smear of red lipstick crossing it. She stares at it for a little while. "Did we forget to pay you?" she says finally.

"It's not that." Mike takes a breath, watches the water curl in that pot on the stove. "It's your husband. You can leave him. I know he hits you." Every syllable thuds in a careful enunciation.

Mrs. Klacken stands with her mouth open, then she turns to the stove and pokes into the pot with that big spoon.

"There's this shelter, the women's shelter, it's pretty nice actually—I know where it is because sometimes a group I volunteer for brings them stuff. They'll help you out, at least with the first bit. Or maybe just give you some time to think."

Mrs. Klacken pokes harder into the pot of water, then leans her face over it until her head is lost in steam.

"We can go right now if you want. Before your husband gets home." Mike only has his bike but figures she'll want to take her own car. Patty can pick him up later.

She turns around to look at him. "What the hell are you talking about? Get out of my house."

"I know he hits you."

She slinks down a bit so that her back is curled and her shoulders are high against her ears. "I'll call the police." Her body pulls tighter, tenser with the words. Steam has turned to watery rolls, creeps down her cheeks to swing, dripping off her chin.

"Come to the shelter with me." Mike reaches around his boob to slink his hand out to her.

She flinches, bounces back and away from him, toward the stove and knocks her elbow on the boiling pot, hard. There's splash and a sizzle. "Shit." She claps her other hand over a quick-blooming burn.

"Are you okay?" Mike jumps another step toward her, but she darts sideways out of his reach.

"I'm fine. You should leave." Her voice is getting higher. "Before my husband gets home."

She twists her arm to see the burn, which is red and shiny. Then she blots it with the tail of her shirt and turns to the sink to run her arm under cold water. Her shirt has pulled up in back, with the blotting, and Mike can see a bruise, a green one, nebulous, hovering above her waist.

"He hits you."

"He does not." She leans far over the sink to get the elbow under the faucet.

"I can see the bruise on your back."

She faces him—Mike straightens—and the shirt drops to cover the bruise. "There's no.... So what?" Then she's focused again on the water running over her arm, dripping the length of it and splashing the floor. "Why don't you mind your own business?"

"I just want to help."

She pulls her arm from the sink and shakes it. "Do you really think I'm going to leave this house with someone like you?"

Mike's shoe clicks on the floor, rattles, then stops, and he holds still. "I could change clothes."

They are facing off then, staring straight into each other's eyes. She's got a fierce look to her, skinny and shiny-faced and hair all frazzled.

Then a sudden hiss as the water on the stove boils over. "Shit." With a towel, she lifts the pot off the burner and pours it into a colander in the sink. The pasta rolls out in a sticky, overcooked wad. "Shit." She lifts the colander from the sink and dumps the spaghetti clump into the garbage. "You should go."

When she looks at Mike again, it's at his chest instead of his face. She's lasering a hole in the right orb until he turns away and walks from the house. He pauses outside the front door. If he could stay longer, just give her some time, maybe she'd come around. Then he hears the bolt sliding and knows his chance is gone.

Mike scoops his bike onto the sidewalk just before Mr. Klacken pulls into the driveway. Mike puts his head down and crosses the street. Then he clamps his wig into place, clips in the shoes, and wobbles out of the neighborhood. It's much later, and much darker, than he ever stays on the road, but he needs some wind tonight, something to lift his spirits, remind him what Boobman is all about. There are no headlights on his bike, but it has reflectors. And Patty has sewn reflective strips into his spandex.

So instead of winding through the Klacken neighborhood into his own, Mike loops onto Bruce Road. He'll ride over this stretch, then fly through the closed and darkened park.

His boobs. He'll tell you they are soft and light and bouncy. And firm and solid and pretty much unbreakable. But, no, he won't tell you what they're made of.

He's back alive on his bike, in the wind, boobs rolling and curls billowing. The shapes are dark but dragging out sideways, morphing into demons. Melanie Klacken was afraid. But Mike doesn't know if it was him or if it was her husband she was scared of. The lights are sharp pinpoints at some distance, globes of yellow fire from others. Or if Mike got it wrong about him hitting her. But, no, he doesn't have it wrong. He's sure of it. The zip of the road, the wash of headlights that come upon him, they leave him dripping with light.

Halfway down Bruce Road, flying over the smooth asphalt—there are the kids, heading the opposite direction, approaching fast. Mike takes the shoulder and holds steady. They'll see who he is, since the lights are good here. The kids take a swerving swipe at him, but not close. The guardrail is between them. He feels lopsided, pulling so slightly off-center.

There are no cars on the road after they pass. Mike takes the left lane and hugs the center guardrail. He's spinning around the last curve, feeling his way into the wind, still thinking about Melanie Klacken, but riding the streetlights.

The kids are behind him again, out of nowhere. He doesn't know how they got turned around so fast. From the left lane, he can't bail into the grassy ditch. He has to hope they mean no harm. They're on him quick. He tries to hold but loses his nerve, wobbles right, and catches the front bumper with the outside point of his ankle. He tips over the guardrail. The bike flips up, tires still spinning. A bra strap catches on the metal and snaps loose. He tucks his head. His legs cartwheel while his arms protect his face. Two rotations, maybe—it's hard to tell. His wrist tangles in the spokes for a second, before the bike tears free and flips the rest of the way across the road. His bike catches the wind like a sail and lifts up up up, then drops into the ditch.

If he'd just held steady. He thinks it as he flies. Those kids couldn't have nudged him over if he'd held steady.

He picks himself up. There are only a few tatters of skin left on the outside of his calf and thigh. He looks at it exactly once, but, after seeing the condition, decides to keep his head up. His left wrist hurts and is swelling, too. Still, it doesn't feel like any bones are broken, and he can walk if he goes slow. The orbs seem intact, but squeehawed, and jiggling out of rhythm. They're lopsided from the wallop they gave to the ground. The wig ripped off with the bike. It's crushed, so he wads it in his cleavage. Mike's head is cool and tingly in the fresh air.

The wheels won't turn on the tangle of metal that used to be his bike, so he scrapes it about a mile and a half along the shoulder of Bruce Road then six blocks to his house, chalking out a smear on the sidewalk. The wind whips over the street and fluffs up a few hangnail tatters of skin on his calves.

Patty is still up. After a gasp, she sits Mike down on one kitchen chair, then lifts his foot up onto another. Mike picks at the wig in his hands, pulls grass and pebbles from the curls, while Patty sponges his leg with a wet cloth. Dirty, bloody water pools beneath them on the linoleum. Mike pulls his focus back to the wig, twists it around his fingers. Patty has tweezers out, pulling stones-and-tar-and-grass-and-glass, ever-so-slowly, from his thigh.

"I can fix the wig, too," she says. The curls are hardly blonde anymore, they're matted with so much dirt, and hardly curls with his pulling at them. "Just let me take care of this leg first."

Pebble after pebble comes clear in the tips of Patty's tweezers. Mike keeps squeezing the wig with one hand.

"Okay, Honey." Mike says. "I love you."

"Also, Mike, I'm worried about your wrist."

Mike's wrist is motionless, crooked in his lap. He hadn't noticed.

Patty puts her hand beneath it, so gently. "I'm almost done. Then we'll head in and get that looked at."

Mike nods, and, with the movement, it's not his wrist

that feels strange but his shoulder. The weight is not right, it's uneven. He twitches and twists, tries to ease back into place.

Patty's eyes widen.

Mike feels a whiz, a current, a wetness. There's no noise, just a silent suctioning. He looks down at his chest and his bony knee appears, slowly, just behind the sculpted nip, then pops all the way into sight as his right boob shrinks, sags, and then flaps, empty, against his belly. The boob is blown, popped, dripping down his side, destroyed.

Snow White Alive

When I took off my headphones and emerged from my home office, Snow White was passed out on the kitchen floor. Blood forked down her forehead from the part of her hair. Then I saw it didn't start there but higher. A comb was embedded in her scalp, hammered down so it pierced her skull. I tried to pull it loose, but it wouldn't come. I gripped the mother-of-pearl edge of it with both hands and pushed her head away with my slippered foot. The ooze that poured from the hole was not blood. At least not all of it was blood. It was brain juice.

Still, that knucklehead woke right up. She was dazed, but she always was. "I'm fine," she said. "A bit lightheaded." And she mopped up the juice along with the blood and some mud that had been tracked in.

I returned to my work. I was an engineer for the mines. I planned pathways to ore, signed off on new tunnels.

Snow was the same and wasn't the same at all after the comb pierced her skull. She was dazed, yes. She was happy, of course. But sometimes she looked at me, and in her eyes there was the deepest sadness you could ever imagine. When she looked like that, I thought of the blood, the way it ran down her forehead, the way the rivulets forked, then connected.

After the blood, I saw the synapses. I *saw* them, inside her brain and inside mine. Explosions marked pathways from thought to thought. Her thoughts. They snapped with mine like a lightning bolt. A spark, a web, a bright connection. Then dark again, but seared behind closed eyes.

Her brain juice on my hands. Did I wash them well?

She kept cleaning. She always cleaned. And she talked to those birds, those squirrels. She knew their language. She always did. Or did she? When the sadness hit her eyes, the animals stopped talking to her. The toads, the birds, the deer and rabbits.

The lightning struck, and it was Frankenstein and his monster, howling. She pushed her thoughts to me. It was a moment of revelation.

I warned her about the peddler woman whose shadow I had seen through the window, who fled as I pulled the comb from her head, who must have been the queen. I warned that she would make another attempt. But my warnings were weak. When I spoke of it, Snow White's eyes weren't sad but serene. She patted my hand.

I worked from home then, drawing diagrams of mines on the computer. She dusted my keyboard, over my shoulder, as I typed. I planned tunnels, remotely programmed the equipment. Her arms were smooth and warm, and the chemicals in my body surged at a whiff of her body's chemicals.

Then I saw her sad eyes reflected in my screen. I torqued my neck, and when the lightning flashed from her brain to mine, from the brain juice leaked on my fingers, I thought the word *trepanation*. And I googled it.

A free-floating sensation. A brain is uncaged. Encased in the tomb of the skull—it limits us. A crack, a piercing, and then it is free.

I didn't hear the peddler come with the ribbons. It must have been the queen. I emerged to eat my lunch that Snow White always made, but there was no lunch and she was on the floor. Her neck was wrapped in rainbow colors, sparkling ribbons. The skin of her neck bulged through the silk. Her eyes were popping from her head. Her mouth was gasping. Her tongue was the wrong color and sticking out.

I jumped for a kitchen knife. The one I grabbed was too big for the task, but the task was urgent, and I cut through the ribbons. I sliced her neck as I did it but not in a crucial spot. She could breathe again, and I ran for bandages.

She couldn't speak right away. I looked at her eyes to see if there was light in them, if she was okay. And there was sadness there, then the firing of synapses. They zapped from her brain to mine. I felt it in the brain juice in my fingers. I saw it in a flash of lightning.

The lightning, the howl, the revelation. There was a glowing fork, a way, a path. She knew it, and she showed me. But the flash was too quick. I couldn't grasp it.

After that, she cleaned up the mess, the scraps of ribbon, so lovely, and the blood that made starbursts on the wooden floor. Such a beautiful color. She swept the floor and then scrubbed it on her hands and knees.

She twittered with the birds, danced with the spiders. When the bunnies hopped through the kitchen, she hopped, too. And even when the house was clean, she never ceased wiping and polishing and sweeping. And singing and twittering as she did so. She didn't talk anymore. The words of her songs had turned to la la and fiddle-dee-doe, bum-de-bum-bum, yeah-yeah.

One day I went to the mines. I had to watch my plans in execution. But I knew they would work. Those bland machines, those tunnels, and the hardhats and pickaxes. Properly tortured, the earth spewed its insides.

When I returned, she was convulsing on the kitchen floor. Foam dripped from her chin. I stuck my fingers down her throat, stretched them long and grasping for the apple. She vomited, and the bile burned the skin of my forearms. She retched again and again, and it brought chunks of food, or sometimes it was a raspy hiss that filled the room and smelled worse than the vomit.

Her eyes were open, but she didn't seem to be conscious. She threw up blood. Then bits of organs, bloody, with veins throbbing in them. She threw up her own intestines. A bit of lung. Her liver, her heart. She kept going. The woodland animals watched through the windows.

Before her eyes closed, she looked at her organs centrifuged around her, then at me. The lightning flashed to me, the green monster sat up, and there was a howl, a roar so deep it went on forever, but it didn't come from her mouth or her lungs. She was propped on her hands and knees, and then her arms buckled and she was mush. I listened for a heartbeat, but her heart was beside her, one point in the bloody spiral that wrapped us. Her chest had deflated. Even her nose had collapsed, and her face sagged. She was a sack of skin with eyes and hard parts where the larger bones hadn't passed.

She was dead. I couldn't fix that.

She was in pieces. That I could fix.

I sorted her intestines by size, and then I found a needle and some thread. I stitched them into a long cord that I wrapped like a ball of yarn. I didn't know the order of the parts that spun out around me. But I pierced the organ bits with my sharp needle, and blood oozed, which seemed like a good sign. Veins and arteries were tangled, but I worked out the knots, then tunneled them through the sleeves of her arms and legs. I stacked bones and affixed muscle to them. The muscles were sticky which I hadn't expected but used to my advantage. It was like stuffing a teddy bear, but the position of the fluff seemed more important. Or maybe it didn't matter at all.

The task took days and nights. I couldn't sleep with her splattered there, so I kept stitching, kept puzzle-piecing. She'd been making a thick stew, or a thin one that grew thick over the days, and I drank it from the ladle when I was hungry. My hair became sticky with her blood. Behind dead lids, her eyes seemed to pulse. I remembered their sadness. I remembered the lightning that flashed and the synapses. The smell was getting worse.

When her body was one piece again, not like a person but like a doll, I hammered together a coffin. For the lid, I used the storm door because it had a window. I'd worked so long to stitch that body together that I wanted to see it. And I dragged the box with the doll of a person out of the house and up a hill.

I was too tired to dig a grave. I was too tired to drag my own body down the hill to my bed. I collapsed beside her on the hill. I fell asleep.

I woke to thunder. I woke to rain. When the lightning flashed, it was her brain meeting mine and the juice of her brain on my fingertips. The synapses flashed with the lightning.

She lifted from the wooden box. She shattered the glass window of the storm door. She sat up. Then she stood. I hadn't even kissed her. She was alive.

Acknowledgements

It's dangerous to let people know how much they mean to you. It might scare them away. But I will be brave.

Many people helped make this book. Some helped by reading drafts of stories. Some helped by supporting and encouraging me as a writer and a human being. Others inspired the stories by being their strange and splendid selves. I can't name everyone, but let me try to thank a few.

I am extremely grateful to—

Emily Flamm, especially, especially.

Erin Kate Ryan, just as especially.

Teachers of astounding talent, Tony Earley (who first made me think I should write stories), Maud Casey, Emily Mitchell, Eileen Brodmerkel.

The Moby Dickers, one already especiallied and Susan Pagani and Samantha Johns.

Everybody at the University of Maryland who taught me or influenced me or funded me—or just listened to me. Particularly Anna Rowser, but never to forget Taylor Adams, Susan Anspach, Alexandra Calaway, Carolyn DeCarlo, Eva Freeman, Jesse Freeman, Carlea Holl-Jensen, Katherine Joshi, Daniel Knowlton, Lutivini Majanja, Jenna Nissan, Mary Lynn Reed, Jesse Ritz, Kshiti Vaghela, Vanessa Wang, LiAnn Yim, Heather Marléne Zadig.

Other writers who helped me through important and dreadful drafts. Most of all Alesha Handy, Negeen Darani, William Moore, Virginia Borges, Ron MacLean, Roseanne

Pereira, Kathryn Savage.

Everyone at Veliz Books, especially Sean Bernard.

All of the journal editors, readers, and staff who took a chance with these stories before they entered the book, including those at *Alaska Quarterly Review, Cincinnati Review, Metázen, Moon City Review, Southeast Review, Sundog Lit, Water~Stone Review,* and *Yemassee.*

The folks at the Loft Literary Center, Vanderbilt University, Grub Street, and the Minnesota State Arts Board for supporting me, welcoming me, and helping me write better.

And thanks to my family (*all* of you) for making me weird.

About the Author

Allison Wyss has a thing about body modification, dismemberment, and fairy tales. Her stories have appeared in *Alaska Quarterly Review*, *Cincinnati Review*, *Water~Stone Review*, *Moon City Review*, and elsewhere. She has an MFA from the University of Maryland. Some of her ideas about the craft of fiction can be found in a column she writes for the Loft Literary Center, where she also teaches classes. *Splendid Anatomies* is her first book.